Areej Gamal is an Egyptian writer, translator, and film critic. *Mariam, It's Arwa* won the Sawiris Cultural Award for Emerging Writers in 2021. She has published three collections of short stories and won first prize in the Goethe Institute Cairo's short story competition. This prize-winning story was translated into German and another of her stories was published in English translation in *An Alternative Guide to Getting Lost*. *Mariam, It's Arwa* is her first novel and her first book to be translated into English.

Addie Leak is an editor and literary translator from French, Arabic, and Spanish. Her work has appeared in such outlets as *Words Without Borders*, *The Common*, *The Huffington Post*, and *The Georgia Review*. She has also translated *A Mask the Color of the Sky* by Bassem Khandaqji. She received her MFA from the University of Iowa in literary translation, was a Fulbright scholar, and currently lives in Amman, Jordan.

This translation was commissioned as part of the
Sawiris Cultural Award for Best Novel by an Emerging Writer,
an initiative of the Sawiris Foundation for Social Development.

Mariam, It's Arwa

Areej Gamal

Translated by
Addie Leak

First published in 2026 by
Hoopoe
113 Sharia Kasr el Aini, Cairo, Egypt
420 Lexington Avenue, Suite 1644, New York, NY 10170
www.hoopoefiction.com

Hoopoe is an imprint of The American University in Cairo Press
www.aucpress.com

ISBN 978 1 649 03513 4

Library of Congress Cataloging-in-Publication Data

Names: Jamāl, Arīj. author | Leak, Addie translator
Title: Mariam, it's Arwa : a novel / by Areej Gamal ; translated by Addie Leak.
Other titles: Anā Arwá yā Maryam. English
Identifiers: LCCN 2025050132 | ISBN 9781649035141 hardback | ISBN 9781649035134 trade paperback | ISBN 9781649035158 epub | ISBN 9781649035165 adobe pdf
Subjects: LCGFT: Novels | Fiction
Classification: LCC PJ7940.A4386 A8613 2026

1 2 3 4 5 30 29 28 27 26

Designed by Mahitab el-Safty

To Jabbour Douaihy and Abbas Khadir
And to Noémie

Those were ordinary days, filled with disappointments like Christmas gifts, disappointments at work, in friendship, in love, climbing up the stairs, down the stairs, crossing crowded streets and empty ones, my imagination dim and not yet able to create; I pursed my lips and fixed my eyes on the ceiling and sleep came, I slept sixteen hours without a single dream, without changing position, greeting the world and bidding it farewell on my back; I examined bus drivers' faces, and my lips moved without the word "Tahrir" even coming out, I ignored my reflection in the plastic window of the microbus, my pulse dropping, speeding up, as we approached Abdul Monim Riad Square. I listened to the sound of wheels on asphalt, the yells of the street vendors, and I didn't relax until I knew there were no demonstrations, no alarm in people's faces, no smell of blood because still, anytime I had to walk near the museum, my ears strained to hear sounds from outside my field of vision, from around the bend in the sidewalk. After the scene with Central Security and the word "down" repeated, I could no longer tell hallucination from reality, shots fired, people running toward me screaming, I could've been dropped by a rubber bullet, could've been arrested just for entering the damn area and left to die in detention, death seemed mandatory and inevitable; I saw officers rape female protestors, and horses trained to harass girls like me who entered the circle by accident; not once did I manage to separate fear from reality, I just kept walking, fighting to keep from staggering so I wouldn't seem drunk. Those were long, ordinary days, their only distinguishing moment *her* coming toward me, confident; in a white shirt and jeans, she crossed the street, her eyes fixed on my face and not the frenzied traffic, I don't know how she sensed my fear of crossing to the other side, I don't know how she knew me, her pale face and wispy hair indicating every possibility at once, her feet moving quickly as though she were trying to save a baby and the baby was on the other side of the street. I waited and watched the world pass by in the slow rhythm of a dream as she came up level with me, I buried my nose in the scent, sweat and perfume and something that spoke of the body, looked into her eyes as she approached and the image crystallized; she took my hand in hers and turned me around, two ballet dancers in a magical leap backstage, no one saw us crossing, the voice of the world died away, the moment seemed eternal; I wanted to lie down and sleep, smiling. She handed me off to safety and turned one final time, her eyes drifting across my speechless mouth; she kissed me on the cheek and left, and the voice of the world came back as she receded out of sight into the area around the museum. Those were ordinary days, filled with disappointments like Christmas gifts, disappointments at work, in friendship, in love, climbing up the stairs, down the stairs, crossing crowded streets and empty ones . . .

My life started before I was born. Mama sat on a solitary chair in the exact center of the room, as if she'd measured out the space and chosen her spot carefully. She was afraid she wasn't pregnant, her face tinged with yellow, her eyes unfocused and on her head the long brown hijab she wore to pray, to beseech God, and meet strangers. For the past few nights, when Baba had rolled off of her, he'd left her hungry, but she didn't say anything, thinking, *Well, at least I'll have a baby*. He got up, heedlessly leaving his children in her womb, and as has always happened, many of them died—many, many of them—and only I survived.

As Mama sat frightened in that empty room, she gazed at the ceiling and tried to talk to God; she didn't know yet that I'd survived. She pressed her arms against her chest, humbling herself to speak to God, who she thought was in the ceiling, clinging to him more than ever, calling out weakly: "You're all I have." She wasn't seeking sympathy. "Could you really leave me?" She was asking in earnest, unable to bear it if the answer was yes. That's why she cried on the words "leave me," and I cried with her in the womb; I remember it perfectly because it was the first thing that happened after I was created: Mama cried because she didn't know how to get pregnant with Baba's child. She kept her hands pressed against her chest, then raised her upturned palms toward her mouth, then decided to humble herself further by pulling her legs up onto the chair, her knees pressing against her breasts. She tried to forget the room and its emptiness, and without prompting, she suddenly thought of Mariam, the mother of Jesus, maybe even saw her, a vision passing through her mind as she sat folded up, pleading, lost.

Arwa, that's the first image I have of my mother, an image of grief my presence didn't replace with happiness. How could I tell her God had heard her and answered? *I'm here, Mama*, I watched the scene from afar, like a convict through the bars of her cell, I let it trickle into my blank slate of a mind, and I could never forget it. Mama fixed her thoughts on Mariam: "Mariam, you're a mother—please let me be a mother, too." How to seek help from someone God can't refuse: "Mariam, tell him to give me a gift, and I'll name the gift Mariam." That's when Mama named me Mariam, and maybe when she made me Mariam, in a moment of madness when she would have pleaded with God for anything, promised everything, as if drunk. "Give me a daughter, and I'll name her Mariam."

She was still looking at the ceiling in supplication when she felt, as she later told me, that she saw God—really—and heard the sound of Mariam's brief laughter, the kind that accompanies good news.

Mama fell in love with me before I was even born, and that made up for the miserable beginning, as you'll see. Exactly a month later, Mama took a test, and she was finally pregnant. She waited till Baba got home from work and served him his supper; she sliced his bread, chilled his water, smiled at him, smiled with love, tried to get him to meet her beautiful eyes. He didn't; he turned away from her slightly, losing patience, as though threatening to go back to his meal if she didn't start talking, so she told him. She explained everything that had happened, the wishing and begging, Mariam's laughter and the ceiling through which she saw God; she wanted to tell her miracle to the world, which for her was just that narrow room and Baba; she would have loved for him to believe with her, she kept going over it and adding details, and he remained quiet, his mood unchanged, forcing himself to be patient until Mama stopped talking. Then he turned back to his food and said with a simplicity at odds with her reverence and gravity, "I want a boy," and then he was silent.

He left her to gather up the burst balloons of her wishes, one by one, alone, and stood, asking for tea. His declaration had summoned a number of voices, erasing Mariam's voice and her quick laugh. The ticking clock suddenly seemed very loud, and for long days after, Mama heard the hands of the clock whispering, "A boy a boy a boy." Her shoulders slumped, and she walked slowly, falteringly toward the bathroom door, where Baba was washing up, "Okay, I'll pray again, for a boy." She wanted to appease Baba by sharing in his wish from a distance, but things don't work that way with God. Deep down, she knew the first prayer had taken root; if she changed it now, the prayers could get scrambled and the wishes scattered, and nothing at all would end up happening. When she went into the kitchen, hurrying barefoot to prepare the tea, she addressed the kitchen ceiling, asking him to give her Mariam but, "after Mariam, a boy."

It wasn't just that her dreams were closing in around her; so was the miracle of finding me. The world before her shrank, an insect she'd stepped on and forgotten about who then forgot her; her heart sank, and she lost faith that Mariam had ever laughed in this world.

But I was there, Arwa, alone in the dark, waiting to come out into the world and convince Baba that I would love him like a boy, and convince Mama that she didn't have to be sad because everything that day had been real. The first time I stood up without her help and started to bumble around the narrow room, she told me, "I dreamed of you from the very beginning." Her eyes were shining, the way mine do when I talk about you.

Before going to bed that evening, Mama said to Baba, "Sleep with me tonight," but he paid her no attention, turning away from her, away from her heart, putting a pillow between his legs and saying, "I'm tired." Mama thought he was sulking because, like her, he knew I was a girl, so she fired off a defense: "How could we bring a boy into an apartment this tiny?" She continued animatedly when he didn't answer, "We'll have a boy later, when we have a bigger place." Mama didn't hear Baba's voice again that night; she fell asleep on her back, with no nightmares or pleasant dreams, reassured that at least her genes would live on.

Do you know how I lived inside Mama all those months, Arwa? Like a bird! Constantly fluttering, floating in her belly with wings like silk, unbreakable, every day calmly cultivating the earth that had sprouted nothing but me, aware that I made her uncomfortable. I watched the wide world from afar, from its core, without asking reality for anything. In Mama's depths, I flew, and time passed like it does in dreams, there was no time, just me and Mama and Baba; of all the siblings that came and went, none remained, we were the movie's main characters.

How many times did I see Baba embracing Mama, his face flushed with emotion, and see Mama get angry and scowl before giving in. I was lodged next to her liver and moved away as he knocked a few times against her womb and poured out a tinted liquid, then returned to my place when he quieted.

As Mama's belly grew, my presence became a foregone conclusion in the eyes of the world, no magic, just another being added to the endless number of beings born and living and dying like the ones before them were born and lived and died, without the universe holding its breath or counting its losses to distinguish them from victories. I was in no hurry to come out, nothing was finer than my life there, I knew everything, or at least I thought I did, stories and wisdom and feelings, knowledge that didn't hurt because it wasn't concrete; I was only lacking in a single area whose existence I couldn't fathom any more than I understood its overwhelming influence: a knowledge of endings.

The end came when Mama's body started to cast me out, as though it hadn't fed me and rocked me to sleep and taught me to fly all that time, it cast me out when

I was safe, going about my business with a smile, suddenly and without warning. I'd been watching Mama's dreams on the silver screen, the same as always, drawers and spools of thread and little kids without legs playing, without knowing they didn't have legs, cans of Pepsi, and little girls who were carbon copies of my mother being caught up by the sky as they played. Nothing to prepare me for the violence of my expulsion when I exploded into the outside world.

Arwa, I'm sad to say that Mama tricked me.

I started sliding down under the influence of a powerful force that only became stronger when I tried to resist. I tried to hold on. I wrapped my wings around the liver, attached myself to the top of the stomach, bitter regret strangling me. I ruined the machinery I'd kept watch over. If I were a wolf, I'd have howled from the pain. But of course I didn't howl, I just kept sliding, unable to believe that God, who'd placed me in paradise, was now ripping me out of it. Blood and the sound of Mama's screams forced me to give in and forget about the past; Mama didn't want me there anymore.

The film reel went fuzzy, my head started spinning, and I couldn't bring myself to keep looking; noise filled my ears.

That was the true beginning, it seems. I was born.

I was no longer a bird; I'd lost my wings in the futile battle inside. I opened my eyes gradually; the vast darkness of the womb I'd been able to see so clearly in dissolved, and the glare of neon lights attacked. I still don't know why they tortured me like this, like they do all children everywhere, with no concern for the brand-new lenses I saw through. I kept squirming away from the light and kept crying; this was the world I'd watched from afar, and I thought it was simple and plain, Mama was the most beautiful thing in it, and I was with her at last, but I still felt a growing need to escape and go back where I'd come from, to protest and say I didn't want to be born now, but since I was still wordless, I just cried in the hope that they would understand and send me back; I imagined it was possible to go back and possible for them to understand me.

The nurses' faces filled my photoreceptors; they were laughing and smiling cheerfully, passing me around for kisses, mischievous, ignoring all this crying that demanded to be acknowledged; they were elated by my arrival and my acquiescence in their wingless arms, an elation that had nothing to do with me: it was simply the way of the world in spite of everything. They were elated with the kind of elation made to be forgotten when people go to sleep at night, the kind made only to be forgotten. And because I studied their faces carefully while I cried, I knew that this new world was stupid, malicious, and quick to forget, and I had to accept that it would never let me go back home.

I screamed for the first time in a hospital called al-Yamama, in the arms of the doctor, with the nurses gathered around us. As you might expect, Baba didn't come, he didn't pluck me eagerly from their hands, so I grew up a little and left off crying. I quietly allowed them to give me a warm bath and dress me in winter clothes, and, after that, they took me to Mama in her hospital bed, and, Arwa, that moment was sacred; I want to delay the pleasure of telling it the way we delay our pleasure together.

The al-Mutanabbi Street souk in Riyadh was big, the biggest market I've ever walked through to this day, with displays of dresses in colors whose names I didn't know, precisely wrapped rolls of machine-woven fabric, shops that sold children's toys, and booths around them filled with plastic dolls that smiled and spoke the few words they knew over and over, in a language I didn't understand that still delighted me: sometimes their eyes would light up or they would say "Mama," without prompting any response from the other dolls. They were girls; I rarely saw a doll that was a boy, or if I did, I forgot. They were the same height as me, or a little shorter; Arwa, I looked like I could be their sister.

Then there were the goldsmiths' shops that the women converged on, women who craved gold and were forced to curb their lust for the sake of the little palms they held tightly in their own, keeping them from wandering away and getting lost or kidnapped.

We were making progress: by then I could walk and talk, and when I stood up, I reached the level of Mama's belly exactly; I understood speech and could translate all these crowded human images into short, distressed phrases that went out to ears that of course didn't hear them. Mama held my hand as she walked, covered up with a black abaya, and we were alone; Baba would come around the time the shops closed, which was when he left work, and would wait for us by the entrance. Beside me,

Mama looked at the rows of goods that changed with each new step, and I took turns looking up at the dark sky and at the dolls lying in wait for me on either side.

Where exactly did the sound come from? When did it start, and how did it shatter the calm of the market? I didn't know, but it started getting louder, as though the sun were suddenly rising at night for the first time since the universe began, and when the sound turned the souk upside down, it made me drop Mama's hand.

I'll tell you, if the souk was the world, that sound knocked it off its axis, it happened like it does in nature, suddenly but organically. The sound was the keen, piercing scream of a group of women on the street who happened to be dressed in black, the color of mourning; it was a fleeting sound that didn't feel fleeting to me.

A mother had lost her little boy, seduced by dolls that said "Mama" or action figures that lifted their weapons, or something else I didn't know about, and the agonized screams turned into wailing when the loss was confirmed, and for a very short time it managed to silence the rising murmurs of other shoppers before it was replaced by words confirming the loss: "Oh, the poor dear," "May God make it up to her," "They took him." I turned away from the voices that frightened me and forced me to look up to the sky for help, only to see the darkness as I'd never seen it before, and I strayed from Mama and was forced into the role of the lost boy, I turned around and around like a compass that had lost its center point and broken a leg and begun to limp through the market. The screaming and wailing suddenly issuing from all the shops pushed me farther into the souk.

The footage kept rolling as I wandered about in circles in the mazes that appeared out of nowhere and swallowed me up, or at least appeared from a place I was too small to take the measure of, and, Arwa, the mazes were safe, or at least they tried to seem that way to lower my defenses. In truth, it didn't even occur to me to be defensive; I just remembered my golden early days and thought, I'll go back to flying, like an earthly bird, and the sound neither disappeared nor diminished, and the dolls' eyes kept shining at me kindly.

The game I played with my memory was getting good; I'd closed my eyes and given in to it when I was pulled back to reality by Baba shaking me, rattling my brain to shock me awake. I knew I'd lost, but my body tried to resist on its own, tried to continue roaming. I came back from the dream against my will and found that the sound had dissipated; the market was once again awash in its customary murmurs. The women were lusting after gold in the goldsmiths' shops, and the children were getting bored of the big market. Baba stared at me silently, visibly wanting to ask when I would stop causing him problems, then he pushed me toward Mama; I ran to her and joyfully shouted, "Mama!" I wanted to say, "Did you miss me?" and tell her proudly about going from darkness to light and vice versa, but instead she slapped me, like someone quickly hammering in a nail to catch it before it falls. My teeth felt thick in my mouth, and I tasted blood and knew how bad it was, this thing that happened because of me: bad enough that no one would forgive it.

I smiled to try and manage the heat emanating from my cheek; I was embarrassed to cry in front of all these dolls and children and the night. I raised my chin with difficulty to tell Mama, "I'm sorry"; her face was flushed and scowling, nothing could erase that frown, her eyebrows and beautiful eyes melted into a single, fierce lump of flesh, like an eye in the middle of her forehead, giving me a look I knew, the look from the day I was born, when she took me from the doctors as she lay exhausted in bed. She was grateful because the miracle had occurred, she'd had me, and on the verge of bitter tears because I was the girl she'd wanted. My mother tried to die that day, Arwa, I saw her hold her breath and cried with all my might to calm her dread. Mama didn't die, just continued to look at me as a source of disappointment, one that would chase the person it affected to their grave, in other words, a curse.

1

Baba's name was Muhammad Ali, and Mama's was Siddiqa. I got used to our peculiar life in Riyadh. It wasn't like anyone else's; we weren't like anyone else. Our apartment had just two rooms, without even a formal sitting room; the outer door opened onto the room that was my playroom and Mama's cooking space, our dining room and bathroom, and the second door in the inner wall led to our bedroom and TV and the legless plastic wardrobes with their cloth covers that zipped closed. This was what people found if they got lost and came knocking on our door: me and Mama, in the heart of our daily life.

In another wall, there was a third door, a low one that no grown-up could fit through unless they stooped: the roof door.

Passing through it, we would go to a spot where we could see the other rooftops; we would open the door and take a single step, avoid looking at the terrifying drop to the ground below, and then turn and climb the wooden ladder nailed into the wall until the sky appeared, then the whole world. I never expected it to be like it was.

The roof was barren except for the satellite dishes and the bodies of pigeons that couldn't fly or that died of sheer exhaustion, whose feathers had stiffened and turned dark and whose necks were crumpled. On happy days, we would open the door and climb the ladder. Baba went first, scoping out the area to ensure it was empty of other curious neighbors, with me right behind him. If I stumbled, Mama, following in our steps, would rescue me.

The world appeared in stages with each rung of the ladder I climbed. After being shut up in the box of our boring apartment, I could see the wide, limitless sky. I asked Baba where it ended. "It takes us all the way to Egypt." "And where after Egypt?" "I dunno, I haven't checked." Sometimes, on chilly days, Baba and Mama would busy themselves gathering rocks and bits of scattered wood to make a fire, more for the pleasure of it than for warmth, and I would busy myself trying to imagine what Egypt looked like, that country I wasn't born in, though I spoke its dialect and would have to return there soon.

Those were the days I would ride my bike in circles around them, occasionally losing my balance and screaming with surprise and disgust when I landed on a dead bird; those were the days I talked to God, who lived in the sky, asking him to send me love, a sister, a giant horse, or a great wide sea "every bit as big as your sky" that would be all mine and no one else's. I would repeat my requests to God like he was writing them all down, to be sure he'd grant them in the future, because, as Mama said, "he doesn't forget."

I didn't know he'd send you, Arwa. Tell me: can God take back the sea once it's been given?

But those days ended—that is, the rooftop days—too quickly. The climb wasn't for us, not really; we were inmates like everyone else, possessing nothing more than the narrow prison square below. As for Baba and Mama, they knew better than I did that they had few moments of happiness, that their quarrels had become a natural part of life that could occur anytime, like rain, like loving you, habibti. If reality intruded, we all went back down the ladder, silently praying, to the hole we called our home. I would've preferred to stay alone under the sky to watch the pigeons when they flew or even when they died, so I could keep talking to God. I wanted to skip listening to Mama's stories, which always started after Baba went to sleep and became more intense as the night wore on.

Mama's stories forced themselves into my world. She would sit just in front of the roof door inside the apartment, leaning against the wood, and begin: "Those were dark days . . ." She talked more to herself than to me, or to herself through me, wandering off toward nothing and no one, then returning to me and saying, "You have to know the story of Monkey Island."

"Eat first, or I won't tell the story. Once upon a time, long, long ago, there was a big island. The island was in the middle of the ocean, and the ocean was a thousand seas all flowing into each other. And in this ocean was a single island: Monkey Island. A thousand monkeys lived on it. And every monkey lived by itself under a tree."

"They didn't have homes like our home, Mama?" "No, God broke the mold with ours . . ." "And they didn't have a roof, Mama?" "No, they didn't have roofs, either." "And no baba or mama?" "No, no baba or mama. Eat first, or I won't continue the story. The monkeys had trees, and nothing else. And every monkey had a friend or neighbor. At night, they would stay up late talking about the ocean. How it drowned everyone who tried to get close to it. But they were happy in spite of everything. And their dreams made up for everything they lacked." "And then what happened?"

"One day a monkey said to his friend that the ocean was starting to rise; it was higher than normal, every day about an inch." "What's an inch?" "About the size of your little finger." "What did that mean?" "It meant that the island might sink, and the monkeys might all die."

"Can we get them to walk away, Mama?"

"They can't walk on the ocean."

"So can we ask whoever owns the ocean to do something?"

"God owns the ocean, Mariam, and he didn't do anything."

"So we'll tell the monkeys to go to sleep."

"They did sleep, and they didn't wake up. In a day and a night, Monkey Island disappeared, and all that was left was a story. And since you didn't eat all your food, I won't tell you another one."

I slept, too, and when I woke up, I found that Baba had gotten home from work, like he did every day, but it didn't change anything about the story when he came in looking hopeful and slammed the door behind him. He turned and examined Mama's face as she sat against the roof door and could tell she wasn't mad anymore after their quarrel the day before, that she was better now. He didn't usually ask how that happened; he would just sit down, put his feet on the table, and start up with boring, never-ending stories about work. They talked without taking notice of me as I shivered in the corner of the room, fighting a thousand imaginary wars to get off the island. Surviving alone meant betraying the monkeys, leaving them in the ocean and fleeing, and it wasn't an easy decision.

When you're a little girl living in a rectangular one-room apartment split into two smaller rooms, and that's your whole home, when you rarely see the sun and have no friends or siblings, you can't get away from stories all that easily. Or maybe you can, but only by means of a new story, and sometimes I would forget how to do that. I think people forget that a lot; they forget that escape is even an option. But when the universe is feeling kind, it will remind you how to do it, before the new story gets away from you. That's what happened to set me free from Monkey Island.

When Baba and Mama went to bed, they told me they were going to sleep. "You, too—time to sleep." I said, "Okay," even though I was scared and knew from experience that sleep wouldn't come when I was scared—the fear had to go first. But I held my tongue and went to the couch that served as my bed, lay down under the cover, and waited for them to say something: "Come sleep next to us," or "Come sleep between us," anything that would drive away the fear.

Mama stretched out on the bed first, with only the long pillow that looked like a worm between her and the wall, and allowed Baba to lie down behind her, imprisoning her between himself and the wall, which seemed to give her the giggles, and Baba started laughing at her laughter. All she said to me was "Go to sleep already," and she didn't add anything else. Her face was touching the wall, and Baba put his nose against her neck, fusing his belly with her lower back, his arm reaching over her, all the way around to her breasts. He said something I didn't hear, and Mama gave a strange laugh, and I drifted off.

All three of us were trying to flee a high wave that pursued us, striking every time we moved away. We were just about to drown when I suddenly opened my eyes and stared up at the low ceiling. I got to my feet, sweating, and found the door of the room locked; I was alone, with Baba and Mama outside.

At times like these, I would think of the princess in the Mario game, a little princess with yellow hair wearing a red and white dress. Baba said the princess changed at every level of the game, but we didn't see any other princesses, just this one. By "we," I mean me and Baba and Mama when we took turns playing. Spellbound, I would examine every tiny detail of the virtual princess, and every single time, Mario would fall into the fire, get beaten by the beast, have his prize stolen from him, all because of my awful gaming skills, which refused to improve.

When the television was switched off, the princess would slip out of the game and into my make-believe, and Mario was left alone in the darkness of the mazes, missing out on morning as it dawned on earth.

Kind and silent, she never got sad or angry because of me. Her image was carved into the wooden door that hurt all who entered without permission; I was the only one allowed to see her. She leaned toward me, her eyes soft with affection. I could see her luminous face under the translucent veil that half-covered her forehead, and I blushed thinking about what we would do together, alone in the room; we had to do it fast, before Baba and Mama came back. The image came and went as I desired; I put my lips on her lips, I drew closer and said, "Don't be shy, habibti. I'm your sweetheart, your little girl's father. Come here." I held her and felt the monkeys come back to life and start jumping around in my chest. I gave a start as I tried to hold the princess, to control the image, I squeezed tighter and tighter, I didn't want to leave any space between us. She was the love who understood me; I would follow her, and she would follow me. She was the love who saved the monkeys from drowning and restored their island, took the story back to its beginning.

How was I supposed to put this fire out? I didn't know, and the princess never stopped smiling the same smile, modest beneath her veil, shy and far away, and the fire increased the distance. I hadn't yet learned, Arwa, how lovers put out that fire, so I lost hope and banged my head against the wood, hurting myself, then went back to the couch and cried myself to sleep.

Mama had stories, too, charmless ones; she lived suspended inside them, and when she decided to tell them, it didn't matter whether someone was listening, it was like she was talking to the universe at large. She told me that storytelling was the only thing that could save you from heartache, but I knew it couldn't save you from dying. Mama kept telling stories right up until she died; I'll hear their echoes for the rest of my life. An example: let me tell you the story of the boy called Ali.

Ali was Mama's brother, born after four daughters, making him the youngest in the family. Mama was the second-oldest girl and Ali's favorite sister, my grandfather and grandmother's favorite daughter. Ali was born bow-legged; he loved to play, but it was painful. Ever since my grandmother got pregnant with her first child, she, like my grandfather, had wanted a boy. But the boy came as the last of the bunch, and when he finally did come, he was sickly. They expected he would live out his life dejected and angry at the world and wished they could lend him some of their own health and hope.

No one was allowed to taste the sweets except Ali. No one was allowed to smell the sweets except Ali. There was no one like Ali. The girls burned up with objections; they stayed quiet at first, then expressed their grievances. Ali couldn't eat an entire kilo of sweets by himself—it was so unfair! But what happened was exactly that, unfair. Every day, Ali threw the leftover sweets out the window, laughing. He would swell up with pride and say the birds were going to come eat Ali's food and then sing a song about him, like the misaharati during Ramadan when he came with his drum and called out to wake everyone for the pre-dawn meal.

Mama pressed her back more firmly against the wooden door leading to the roof, then told me, her eyes full of tears, that Ali could've been a singer; he had a singer's dreams.

After ten days of gorging himself on sweets, Ali hated them and the shop that sold them, and of course got sick of his baba and mama, as well. He screamed in their faces, crying and slapping at his legs with his little palms: "I hate you!" That day, both father and mother sobbed until the girl, watching anguished from behind the door, thought they would die crying. She put her hand over her mouth to silence her ragged breathing, to keep them from noticing her there. She felt that she should never, ever forget this image.

Even the image of herself standing behind the curtain, her hair tied back in a single, trembling braid, was branded in her mind. She couldn't forget it, so neither did I.

Ali wanted, like I did when I was trapped inside, to run away from his prison, like the birds that flew away and came back to him as he sat beside the window, unable even to walk like most people. That night, Mama told her sisters what had happened. They laughed and laughed at the image and said "Good!" before sleep carried them off to its realms of freedom, leaving Mama alone in the room with Ali's frailty.

Mama fell asleep with an idea bouncing around in her head, and when she woke up in the morning, she saw it—the idea—practically springing off the ceiling.

Siddiqa went to Ali, whose eyes were silently following the legs of passersby in the street, and said to him, "Want to play with me and my dolls?" Ali didn't answer, like he didn't even hear. "I'll show you how." And without waiting for him, she brought the tribe of dolls from the box in the bedroom and fashioned a family and children for him. Ali enjoyed playing, and when this enjoyment reached its zenith, he started demolishing the dolls one after another; he put them beneath his feet and, exuberant, stomped on them for a full minute.

I didn't know then what a minute was, but I guessed it was maybe the length of a kiss. I imagined the stomping taking place in front of me and asked Mama, "And then what?" She was the only one who cried that time; her baba and mama were proud that Ali was laughing and that he looked happy again.

The girls made fun of Mama, the "idiot" who'd given all her toys to Ali, the "retard," and then forgot what had happened. No one thought to try and compensate her for her loss because Siddiqa didn't ask for compensation. Dolls became Ali's favorite toys; he would go into the girls' room, limping slightly, create families from the dolls hidden under their beds, then rip their heads off and leave the room laughing like a conquering hero. Siddiqa didn't know whose fault it was.

When Mama asked me, as she talked, I felt somehow responsible for all of it and didn't answer.

Ali's sadness moved into the girls' bedroom, and Ali was free; everyone who saw him was surprised and delighted and said "Mashallah!" The girls could never forgive Mama, the one who'd opened the door to all this destruction. After some years, Ali's legs healed. He walked, even ran, in the streets, and he bought a gun and learned to shoot pigeons and other birds. The girls fled the house one by one. Mama ran the farthest; she got married in a foreign land and had me and said to herself she could finally rest.

Did she rest? Of course not. She had me, her first baby, and then she tried, because she'd promised Baba, to have a boy. Baba wanted a boy named Ali, after my grandfather. The boy's name would be Ali Muhammad Ali, and just *imagine* that name engraved on a marble plaque over a doctor's office, or an engineer's. As for me, when Baba mentioned it, I couldn't picture marble plaques over anything but graves. That's how I'd seen them in the movies once; I didn't remember which film.

Baba came in while I was arranging my dolls in a line, like schoolgirls, and broke the line with his foot, sending one of them flying and skidding onto her face. When I looked up at him, his face was red, and his nose was swollen with anger, as if the emotion was trapped under his skin. I forgave him because he didn't mean to do it, then hid the rest of the line in a cardboard box and closed the flaps on them; they were engulfed in darkness, and I withdrew to a corner.

He went into the bedroom, where Mama was. He closed the door behind him, then they came out together. Mama's nose was swollen now, too, and her face was the same color as his. In the time that elapsed between his going in and their coming out, I stayed in the corner with the dolls, my eyes never leaving the door, I don't know for how long.

In Baba's hands was a white envelope, a package from Egypt from my grandfather and grandmother. "Give me the tape player," he said. Mama brought it to him and, stepping away again, suddenly asked me, "Did you eat?" I nodded without thinking and waited, not knowing what I was waiting for.

In the envelope were two reels of recording tape carefully wrapped in a soft, lightweight handkerchief. Baba used a small screwdriver and a few screws to insert the two reels into a cassette tape, then put it in the tape player. That was the only entertaining part. What followed was my grandmother's voice coming from the speakers. It was the story about his aunt again:

> Your aunt is upset that you had a girl. I told her it was God's will, far be it from us to go against him; just wait, and he will give him a boy to make up for it.
>
> Muhammad—you have the right to take another wife, *and* a third one, and a fourth one. A month after our wedding night, your father put his hand on my belly and said, "It's a boy." Exactly nine months later, Sulaiman came. Your aunt is upset; she says we're Sa'idi—we need men to carry on the line. It was God's will for you to have Mariam, okay, and we can't go against God's will. So then the Lord will bring a boy tomorrow. Your aunt sends her greetings and wants to know, why "Mariam"? The girl's name should've been Umm Kalthoum, after me. Isn't it bad enough she's a girl? I told her Siddiqa picked the name, now it's between her and God. I saw your daughter's picture; she looks like her mother. Your father sends his greetings, and asks when you're coming home. Seven years, Muhammad! Your father's afraid he'll die without seeing you again. We're waiting. Take care, bye.

The tape player clicked off as we ate, sitting on the ground. I was as close as possible to my cardboard box to protect the dolls as dinnertime dragged on. Every time I swallowed, food got stuck in my throat, so I drank water—anxiously, because Mama didn't like it when I drank water with meals. We ate in silence; the television was off, and they weren't talking. Baba's face had gone back to normal; he opened his jaw as far as it could go, and it popped, and he didn't look at me. Mama's lips were pale and her face grave, and she didn't reach toward the plate.

Baba's voice came out sounding natural. "I found you a job." "What job, and what about Mariam?" For no reason, Mariam felt even more scared for the dolls. "You're still not pregnant. We're working so we can go to Egypt." "What about Mariam?" Mama said again. Her face was as white as Baba's rapidly emptying plate. I think, Arwa, that Siddiqa was even more scared than I was, for her own doll. "What about Mariam?" "Mariam's bigger now; we'll just lock her in, leave her some food, and you won't be gone that long. What, is she the first girl to be left on her own? If she gets a brother, you'll be too busy for her anyway."

"She's only seven; she'll be scared!" "I'm telling you, you start next week."

That day, Baba drank his tea alone in the bedroom, then called Mama and locked the door behind them, and I fell asleep with my dolls inside the box that blocked out the light. When Mama woke me up, one doll's hair was soggy from my drool, and it made me sad. I told myself it would dry by morning.

Mama's eyes were fixed absentmindedly on the ceiling, and she spoke to herself more than to me: "Don't be upset with me, Mariam." I spoke to the soggy doll: "Mariam's not upset with Mama." "Of course, Mariam could never be upset with Mama. Should she tell the doll a story?" Stories were the only kind of performance I'd ever known, Arwa.

"Which one do you want to hear, sweetheart? The sleeping princess? Okay, I'll tell you."

Mama pulled me against her chest and leaned back on the wooden door like she was getting ready to fly, I leaned back into her belly, and the story started to move between us like a ball: sometimes I caught it, sometimes I threw it. I'd heard Mama tell this story a number of times, but this was the sweetest one by far.

Once upon a time, there was a beautiful princess. Her curls were golden, her eyes were the color of the ocean, and her skin was pale, like Arwa's skin, and mine, and Mama's. This princess had a grandmother who was raising her because her mother had died long ago, of worry and sorrow and waiting for things that never happened. When her mother died, the princess went to live with her grandmother in a cottage in the forest.

The grandmother didn't love the princess the way Mama had loved her; in truth, no one would ever love the princess the way Mama had, but the grandmother *did* love having the princess come live with her: it meant she could claim Mama's gold and fine china, which were the princess's inheritance. The grandmother asked a traveling merchant to prepare a poison she could use to kill the princess in secret, but when the man saw the princess, he loved her, and the task became too difficult; if the princess died, his soul would die with her, so instead he mixed a sleeping draught.

One day, the princess was sitting on the lakeshore, dipping her feet in the spring water as the fish swam up to kiss them, when the grandmother approached the princess and said, "Here, have an apple." The princess trusted her and bit into the most delicious apple she'd ever tasted. When it settled into her stomach, her legs in the water went into spasms, scaring the fish, who didn't know what had happened.

The princess lay strewn across the shore for days, and the merchant hovered about her body, feeling he might die from grief. He knew that what she'd been given was only a sort of anesthetic, that she would come to eventually, but he didn't know how that would happen, and he didn't know how to wake her up or how to forget her.

Then one day, a handsome prince, elegant, with eyes the color of the ocean, came to the forest to fish. When he got close to the lake, he saw something more lovely than being a prince, more lovely than fishing and the fish themselves; it was the princess's hair, long and flowing past her thighs. It had grown as she slept and was now almost as long as the princess was tall. He touched it, then saw her lips; they were open, a dead fish lodged between them. The prince removed the fish, then decided to wash the princess's body with the pure water of the lake. He took off her clothes, not wanting to delay his pleasure. Because of love, the enchantment was broken, and the princess woke at last.

That night, Mariam got the nicest kiss anyone could hope for in a dream.

Those were ordinary days, Arwa, or at least they seemed that way. I met with disappointments like Christmas gifts and invited people to see them, and they came without hesitation: disappointments at work, in friendship, in love, if you can call it that. Life was climbing up the stairs, down the stairs, crossing crowded streets and walking in empty ones, walking without friends or thoughts or goals, my imagination dim and not yet able to create; all these poems I've written with you, about us, hadn't yet been born within me.

You were still a long way off. If I'd seen you arriving at the Cairo airport that day, I would've kept my distance in the metro, and our whole story would never have started; I wouldn't have found something worth feeling. You were at your prettiest, landing in a Lufthansa plane with your German passport, and you knew you might be cross-examined thanks to your foreign looks and nationality: *Don't try to justify your reasons for coming here now, after all this time.* Arwa, you stood in the queue to go through arrivals just like everyone else: *Don't tell them the truth when the officer gets suspicious, asks, "Why are you coming here* now, *Ma'am?"* Instead, what you said, in an English he understood, was, "Work," then briskly slid your passport out from under his hand; he didn't dare object as you raised your eyes to the ceiling, as though threatening to call the ambassador if you had to. Then your eye twitched, and you turned and walked away.

You can be tough when you want to. You pulled one bag along behind you and carried another smaller one on your back in a spacious airport with no beginning or end, walking with your body like a whip, tense and ready to scream if approached, but that visible, deliberate coldness isn't the real you; I was fooled at first, too. When you got back, did Cairo scrutinize you the way I did? Was it pleased with your white shirt and the black sweater you wore over it? Your skirt fluttered as you moved, and the leggings you wore underneath, those lucky things, clung to you. Cairo didn't know how to reclaim you like I did; you walked along like a swan in the ballet hurrying to exit the stage, you stole everyone's attention: the male airport employees who walked behind you as if bewitched, hoping you'd ask them for some service, taxi drivers who started twisting their tongues around the word "limousine" without even knowing, should they be speaking to you in Arabic? And the officers, the officers surveilling who came and who went, at least one of them wished, from the bottom of his heart, to sleep with you.

This in the midst of revolution.

They all forgot the revolution and craved you, Arwa, and that only stokes my jealousy; then I come back to myself and think how, if I'd been there that day, I'd have screamed at them in perfect classical Arabic: "Hear ye, men, officers, hired guns, Arwa doesn't love *you*!" I'd have laughed till I died. Wouldn't that have made for at least one good poem? One sentence to fast-forward past those first moments in Cairo after your break with the city, them rustling along behind you like an army as you looked at your phone, grumbling that it wasn't picking up the local time, ruffling your short hair and massaging your scalp, as if that would give you patience. My beautiful youth, little did you know how you made men pine for you without so much as a glance, focused as you were on a single goal: reaching the apartment on Champollion Street, putting down your bag, relaxing for one hour to go downstairs the next, heading toward what you came for to begin with, your comrades on Mohammed Mahmoud Street. You made your way through the ranks of people on the sidelines, people who, like me, made do with just the whiff of revolution, you surveyed the Central Security Forces and the tanks in the distance, reached a circle, and stood in the center, taking your instrument from your back. Your companions fell silent in surprise and watched as you filled your lungs and played with all your heart, closing your eyes as they stared, their ranks even, waiting for some far-off hope to arrive. You played, and the fog dispersed. A shudder ran through the circle, moving from person to person until it reached the poor souls manning the tank, and they shook and wept without knowing why.

This was a definition of fighter I could only ascertain in theory; I was incapable of song, except in my mind. You remember how we met.

I was in the Cairo University metro station, curfew two hours away; I was sitting down, waiting, my head lowered and my back against a lamppost. The cold buffeted me like a leaf, mercilessly, and I tried to play a game with the women passing, a game of glances whose provocative nature I'd discovered with a ghagariya woman: I would like the look of someone, follow her with my eyes, call out to her silently until she noticed me. I would suddenly feel shy, then take up the game again, look directly at her, telling her with my eyes, "Look at me." They noticed; a lot of them were annoyed, a few returned my gaze, and, in the end, I let them all go.

I was amusing myself with this game when I saw you—and my God! The doors of the metro car, which happened to have stopped just in front of me, opened. I don't remember the crowd, just you planted inside like a traffic light, standing there with your back to the world, which was me; I stole a glance at your vertebrae and noticed your instrument case, which reminded me of my story with the oboe. This upset me, and then you turned, and I saw your face in that moment of turmoil, or all of you, actually, the instrument hiding behind you and looking at me sideways. I was intimidated, as if you'd stepped out of my dreams, a straight-backed body in black and white with short, soft brown hair, a snub nose, light eyebrows, and a sad face that knew something I didn't. When you turned, the way you looked at the things around you, unseeing, mirrored the look your bag gave me. Our eyes met, so I smiled, and you smiled; my smile left when yours did, and I glanced back at you as you glanced at me, just as apologetic and helpless. I called to you without meaning to, followed your movements when you got off the train, beckoned you. You stopped short when you set foot on the platform, and I silently begged you to step away; you inhabited the crowd as one on the verge of losing herself, but I didn't lose sight of you. You repositioned your bag, which was already perfectly placed on your back, your instrument like a monkey clinging to you, only to you, and staring at me. You were forced to contemplate things from a distance, too, you knew all about me, what I'd been doing just then, my game; you sighed, and I knew you'd decided to change course, to sit in a nearby seat; your shoes had barely touched the ground, and I wanted you to come toward me. I moved over a bit in my seat, if you came any closer, I would stand; I wished I could tuck myself away in the earth's pockets, wished that—if it even had pockets—I would fail at doing so, and I waited. I watched you from the corner of my eye and convinced myself you didn't see me and started to act as if I was leaving, as if none of this mattered to me.

You took off the black bag and set it on the ground between your legs, liberating your back, let your exhales succeed each other rapidly in a rhythm I would later memorize as you collapsed atop my body after lovemaking, as if you were jogging or had suddenly stopped. The train in front of us began to move as it left the station, and my eyes remained glued to it till I forgot who I was; I was powerless to stop the past from welling up, just as I couldn't predict when it would happen, all I could do was surrender when it came and watch the events of my life parade before me like a black-and-white film. I could've left at that moment, nothing gained or lost, so what was it I remembered that brought me back to the black bag, which I suddenly found beside me?

"You want to see this, yeah?" Your voice was softer than I'd imagined. "It's an oboe, do you know it?" Hints of ancient mountains and valleys, hints the wind picked up. I was reassured by the mournful gravity in your voice, and my frozen body relaxed; then I registered what you'd said: "Oboe?" I nearly stood up, nearly said, *All right, God, now you're just toying with me.* "Yes, the oboe. Do you know it?" Of course, my tone gave away how well I knew it; this time, I was beaten, and the game became reality. "Why so quiet?" Despite the familiarity of your voice, I admit that your accent was strange; your strangeness only grew in my eyes the more I loved you and the deeper I knew you. I fell silent, not giving any kind of response, and you pulled the instrument case onto your lap like a pet burying its face in your legs and unzipped it with startling speed. I thought, those are a musician's hands, such nimble muscles and tendons, if I'd learned an instrument, my hands would've looked like those. "Are you a musician?" "Yes." You took the oboe from its leather case as if unboxing a new, exciting toy; I wanted to touch it but stopped myself. You held it out to me: "Want to try?" After all that time, was I really seeing it there, in front of me? The oboe was untouchable. "No." I said it quickly and firmly so you wouldn't ask again, then made a request of you, my first and, I thought, my last: "Could you play a little?" So I could round off this meeting with something that would never happen in normal life, ever, hear its timbre with no intermediary, no screens or recordings. Then I came to, registered the people and the metro, and cut myself off, "I'm sorry, I wasn't thinking." "Why are you apologizing? What's the worst that could happen?"

"But it's cold." I wanted us to keep talking aimlessly; you placed the double reed between your lips and began to play, starting high, as if communicating something that had been interrupted, and the sound drew the night to itself. You told me later it was a piece by a Greek composer, Eleni Karaindrou. The oboe launched its notes at the cold like bullets, it drank from your lungs to find its voice, and it tired you out, I could tell, but life rushed into you, burning, and I could see faces flashing before me and disappearing. Your whole body kept pace with it, I could feel it expanding into you, and I was sure I couldn't bear it, this oboe. It was the most incredible performance I'd ever seen in my life, the only real performance, and I expected the music to crack us open, but that didn't happen. The truth that dawned on me was that we meant nothing to the rest of the world, Arwa—aside from us, who cared about two women sitting together in the thick of the revolution and the cold, one playing a wind instrument as little known in Cairo as the oboe? One woman smiling like an idiot and the other puffing away like a musician in the Berlin Opera. My pulse quickened as I watched you openly, unembarrassed, for the first time, freed by your concentration on your instrument. Your unsupported back was straight, as if it, rather than your arms, held the oboe. I envied those confident arms; I saw that they had survived something I had not.

I don't know how long you played; I didn't count the metro cars as they came and went, the way I had before you arrived. I got lost in the music early on, and that night, before I fell asleep, I thought how rare it was for me to lose track of time in public. Curfew might've caught me still outside, leaving me to hurry home, chasing after my fear as fear chased after me, afraid that at any minute I might get shot, but at the time, my awareness of all this had fallen away completely. "You like it?" Your eyes were soft, too, your hand quivering slightly. "It was lovely." "Give it a try." "No." "Why?" I was scared someone might see me and tell my grandmother. "Where do you play?" "On the street, in bars, sometimes at parties, and sometimes here." "Here . . . in the metro, you mean?" "Maybe." You looked around at the metro stop as if for the first time, trying to imagine it as a stage, and I was happy you liked my suggestion. "What about all the people?" I said, then regretted it, feeling I'd spoiled the moment.

"Oh, no worries, forget the people; we're playing for them but also for ourselves. They'll love it." "The police and the military won't." "Why not?" "And then there's the curfew—they could throw you in jail." "Seriously?" "Didn't you know?" "No, I knew. . . but don't worry, we'll run away before they arrest us." "We might not be quick enough. Do you like jail?" "Of course not. Who likes jail?" "They say revolutionaries do, but me, I'm a coward." "No, don't worry, nobody likes jail, not even revolutionaries." "Really?" "Yes, I'm sure." "Do you know anyone who's been to jail?" "Yes." "Who?" "Don't worry about it. I have a foreign passport; that freaks them out here even more than a war would." "So if they caught you, the embassy would get you out of trouble?" "Yes." "But they'd call you a traitor." "So what? Who did I betray?"

I didn't know the answer to your question. Looking into your wide eyes, many things I thought were big and important suddenly seemed worthless. I laughed at my naivety, which was so painfully evident, and that made you laugh, too. "But you liked the music, right?" "Very much." I paused. "Hey, do you have Syrian roots?"

"Why?" "The way you talk . . ." "I've been away from Egypt for ten years." "Where were you?" "München. I mean—Munich, in Germany. I hang out with a lot of Moroccans and Arabs from the Levant; maybe my Arabic is a little dated?" "No, it's nice." "Really, you like it?" "Yeah." Your lips parted in a wide smile as I floundered in my shyness and wished desperately that you would say something, anything, to change the course of the conversation. You obliged. "I think in Arabic, but I live in German; sometimes I try to refresh a little with songs or old letters in Egyptian." "Why did you come back now?" You gave a start and began to put the oboe back in its case, and I worried you would leave; I would've done anything to make you stay. I clarified. "I mean, given the revolution and the curfew and all the violence." "The revolution's what brought me back. They asked me that question at the airport; I couldn't tell them it was because of the revolution, so I told them work. I have an apartment here, and people I love."

Love? The word was like a slap—what did you mean by "love"? Who publicly states that they've come back to their lovers? I watched one train arrive as another departed, and the whoosh of air they stirred up pushed against me, and against you. I didn't know anyone who looked like you; it was impossible to compare you to any familiar image, not in the movies, not in my past, and you didn't realize it, but that scared me. At first, you seemed wolf-like, then your little tilted nose made me think of a bird of prey. I remembered Mama's stories from my childhood and wanted to run away. "Where's the apartment?" "Champollion Street—it's an old place surrounded by workshops. It's still a mess; I just got here this morning and haven't had a chance to clean. Do you live downtown?" "No." "Here, near the university?" "No, I live pretty far off, actually." "Far off where?"

"In El Remaya, do you know it?" "Near Masaken El Dobat?" "Yes." You fell silent, turned away from me, and shifted slightly in your seat, as if we hadn't met, as if I weren't there; you pulled the oboe onto your lap and rocked it like a baby. I was embarrassed to tell you I was an orphan and turned away, too, thinking I would erase all memory of this strange woman whose name I didn't know. The number of people waiting at the stop was dwindling, and fewer trains were coming and going; their drivers would be heading home soon after an empty day, like the passengers, and tomorrow would be empty, too; I felt like life was drifting off toward sleep and thought about all the advantages of going home: the room whose door I could lock behind me, the comforter pulled over my face, the pillows I would press over my ears to block out my grandmother's voice, and of course the dreams. I tried to stop my thoughts before they got carried away, then stood up to go.

If you'd let me go, what happened would never have happened, not that day or in any of the days that followed. Your body rose from its seat, leaving the oboe alone on the bench, and came toward me. "You're leaving?" "Yeah, it's basically curfew; I might not make it home in time." "I mean, you don't have to go home now . . ." You came closer to me, your body blocking my path, your eyes fixed on me, forcing me to take a step back. "My place is nearby, you can hang out there until tomorrow, as long as you're not scared of a little dust." You laughed, then covered your mouth with your hand, almost coyly. "I can't; my grandmother's waiting for me. If she knew I was somewhere she didn't know, she'd be angry." "Let her be angry; the whole country is angry."

I didn't know what to do. "Call her. Can we go look for a phone?" You put your hands on my shoulders, a brief, light touch. "I have a phone, but I don't want to call her; I should go." "You're upset. Sit down, and we can talk a bit more and then go." "I'm not upset." Your breath grew ragged, and then the dam broke, and you overflowed. "I used to live in the Masaken El Dobat neighborhood, years ago; I was there for a long time, and when you said that, I got flustered." It was your last-ditch effort: "I'm sorry." "I'm not upset." "I don't care what time it is, I'll tell you everything later if you want, but please sit down."

But I had to go, Arwa, so I turned to leave, and then you made your first request of me. "Can we walk together, just to the exit?" So we walked together without speaking. Ringing in my head, I heard the clatter of the metro cars, nothing else, and I could no longer see the stairs, or the platform emptied of people. Your image faded, too, and I tried to bring the last few minutes to mind again, to no avail. Why did you walk with me, Arwa?

"Would you like to see me again?" Your eyes weren't pleading; they were simply a gift, innocent and green, and there was nothing like them around us at that metro stop. "Of course," I said, and smiled, then automatically wiped the idea from my mind. You spun around on the pavement as though you were looking for something, or someone, that was lost. "Do you have a phone?" You knew the answer was yes. I wanted to sympathize with your sadness, which had suddenly evaporated, or your drowsiness, I couldn't tell the difference between them. "Yeah—should I give you my number?"

"Yes, just wait a second." You opened the black bag, which was empty save for a piece of red velvet for cleaning your instrument; I stole a glance at the latter, telling myself it was my last. "I'm hoping you have a pen." "Sure." Then "Bye . . ." "Are you okay to get back on your own?" I turned and left you there, sleepy; you smiled again, and I yawned as I exited the station. Your last question, as I'd written down my number, glimmered like a jewel in the night: "What's your name? Mine's Arwa." I repeated it. "Arwa." "Yes, Arwa—and you?" "I'm Mariam." "I want to know you—who are you, Mariam?" Your question and your name, the tone of your voice, these were the last things I remembered as I drifted into sleep, drifting without questions or an identity: how could I respond to your question when I didn't know the answer myself? I'd tried so hard to figure it out; every time I got close, it slipped through my fingers, but God knows I'd tried.

I wasn't born here, but there, far away; I didn't have any siblings or friends, only Baba and Mama, though when I say that, I feel bad for leaving out my dolls, my beautiful dolls who lived in a box just for me, a box the sun never entered. I lived in a room the sun didn't enter, but for no one, really. At first, Mama lived there with me when Baba was at work, until Baba came home at night and stayed there with us until morning. But one day, Baba came home from work and sat down with us on the ground. We were eating, and he told Mama she had to leave me at home and go to work, too; Mama agreed and made it up to me by sitting down with her back against the door to tell me the story of the sleeping princess. She thought I would die of sadness when she left me alone in the apartment.

But by the time she was actually gone, I'd learned from the story—and not only that, but I began to tell myself stories of my own. The apartment was all mine; I took my dolls out of their dark box and spread them out across the floor of the room, one corner for each doll, then gathered them closer to me. The one with golden hair—or whose hair was golden until I got it dark with drool—I took up to the roof with me. I opened the heavy wooden door without help from anyone and climbed the nail-studded ladder straight up to the sky, where I whirled around and around, and the doll would whirl with me, until my arms went numb and the doll slipped from my hand. I didn't stop to get her, she was actually gone, and I told myself she had flown like the birds, like a pigeon, or maybe like the eagle on the Egyptian flag.

They taught me how to write my name, Mariam Muhammad Ali, on the first page of my illustrated workbooks, which had girls who looked like me splashed across their white covers and pages that left blanks for my answers. They told me I had to write all three names at least, and proudly, so that people would know who I was; they told me I was personally related to the great pasha, Muhammad Ali, who founded Egypt, and then they laughed. I didn't know who that was, but I laughed with them and dreamed that my name was just Mariam.

Meanwhile, Baba was dreaming I was a boy; he watched me as I ate and the food got stuck in my throat, then he would go back to eating, speaking up every so often, asking Mama, for example, what the world would've been like if Mariam had been Ali. Mama had regret in her eyes, too, the reasons for which I could see when Baba turned away from us to watch TV. I don't know when Ali became our whole life; when I think about it now, I think my brother was born before I was.

We bought plastic cups with the letter A on them, sheets, hand towels; I would pick out the colors with my parents, and at home Mama would tuck them away in the heavy drawer it took two people to open, where she kept the gold and silverware and china. Guests would visit us, and we'd pull it all out again as a treat, so they all thought Mama was pregnant and would congratulate her and say a prayer. We never corrected them; sometimes I put my pillow under my shirt and came out to tell everyone I was pregnant with Ali, too.

Those were the days Baba used to laugh so hard the sound filled the room, and the guests laughed, too. Ali was going to play and break the cups they were drinking from now, so we would buy new ones for his sake; Ali would be awash in bliss in his expensive cradle, and when he cried, even his tears would be sweet, the kind that don't upset fathers because they're more like a *song* about tears than tears themselves. That scamp Ali would be good at everything, Arwa, a companion for everyone: the childless guests, the ones who'd left their kids at home, and of course those who'd lost their children.

Baba vowed that when Ali was born, he would build him a dovecote on the roof like the one he'd had in Egypt; it didn't matter that the roof wasn't our property, it didn't matter that he could go to jail; happiness would protect him from all misfortune.

Ali's full name was Ali Muhammad Ali, a loyal child of the great pasha, much more than I was; just listen to the music in his name, then to the unevenness of mine, *Mariam*; it's true, it never made me sad because it's simply true, and so I needed to learn to write my brother's name. No one made me do it, Arwa; I was living in the midst of a giant party, and Ali was the guest of honor; I was just happy to be close to him. All that was left was to meet him face to face.

I didn't tell Mama, and I never talked about it with Baba, but I assumed they'd both seen him; his clothes and the way they talked about him were proofs of his existence, and that's why I learned to write his name, because maybe his name would summon him. It's embarrassing, but I had trouble learning then; trying to hold the pen and write tired me out fast. Ustaz Abdallah, my tutor, put on a calm face, his beard wagging, and said, "Mariam's a lost cause" and "her mind is abnormally slow to develop." He repeated "abnormally," at first angrily, then with resignation, and finally with sadness, for Mama's sake, because his words brought tears to her eyes, and he was someone who—at just the thought that she might cry—hurried to make excuses, saying that maybe he'd been late teaching the basics, then shaking his head good-naturedly as if to avoid offending anyone.

Baba didn't particularly care, and once Ustaz Abdallah had left, he told Mama that cash could fix it all when we got back to Egypt. When Mr. Abdallah came the next day, Mama gave him more money and told him to leave names alone for the time being: "Teach her counting; I want her to be able to count on her fingers like other kids." I told him to teach me Mama's name first. He started to, and then I tried, and then we both failed; "Siddiqa" was hard for me. I threw the pen down and started working on counting instead, and the disappointments piled higher. I begged Ustaz Abdallah not to tell Mama; it would kill her, I just knew it.

Mr. Abdallah started laughing then, his beard quivering like the Egyptian flag on the satellite TV channel that played in the morning. He lowered his voice and told me he couldn't lie to her, people my age could already read the papers; then he asked me, what would I do at university? I didn't have an answer; I didn't know what university was, for starters, but I prayed to God I wouldn't have to go there, then I went back to my workbook and tried to read about the grammar of numbers and how they changed by gender and case before Mr. Abdallah's laughter cut me off again and he asked me for the millionth time to call Mama so he could tell her my secret; then Mama paid him even more money to teach me English.

I was suffocating under that roof, Arwa, everything happened in that single room. Imagine doing your homework alone at night, staying up late at the same low table under the same yellow light, working at it until you were done. My homework would have every possible error, but it would be done. I would call Mama: "Come hold my hand, it's shaking!" And Baba would reply with Mr. Abdallah's words, "People your age are reading the papers every morning," then take Mama into the bedroom and close the door behind them.

One night, I opened the door to tell them I *wanted* to be slow for the rest of my life; I'd cried onto my workbook until Mr. Abdallah's handwriting was a blurred mess, and he would punish me the next day—I couldn't take it anymore! Making sure I still looked soggy-eyed and miserable, and with a thin line of blood trickling from my nose, I ran to Mama in the bedroom, bursting in without knocking. Baba would never forgive me for not knocking; Mama would, but she had to pretend, in front of Baba, that forgiveness was out of the question. It was the first time Baba was truly furious with Mariam, and also the last time before he died. The only sign that he saw me was the fact that he yelled at me and sent me out to sleep in the main room: "You're sleeping out there from now on, until I say you can come back!" My life got hard when Baba was angry, so I accepted the punishment and started sleeping in the other room.

When I'd opened the door, I'd thought they were playing, or copying a game they saw on TV, like I sometimes did; Mama was lying underneath Baba with her thighs spread open, and he was planted between them on his knees, trying to get in between her legs. The man on the TV was in the same position, as if he saw Baba and was mimicking him, and on screen, the hole he wanted to penetrate was visible; it looked like a rose, Arwa. That woman was writhing and screaming, without trying to get away, but my mother was quiet, her face red, trying to deprive her lungs of oxygen and stop breathing, and I couldn't see her eyebrows, as though they'd fallen off in the struggle. They stopped when I went in, but the couple on the TV didn't stop.

Baba asked what was wrong with me and jumped out of bed, turning his back to me. I saw his pale white buttocks as he tried to rush into his clothes, and Mama wrenched her thighs shut and held them against her chest, pulling the blanket up to cover her body, distancing herself from me; she tried to calm Baba down and asked me, lowering her voice, "What do you want?" I forgot what I wanted; all I could think about were the princesses in Mario, who made me both want to cry and to hold them. Is this what would've put the fire out? I wanted to know what exactly I was supposed to have done, but I couldn't figure it out; I looked at the TV and felt that pain I still haven't found relief for. The woman was moaning, putting her finger in her mouth and biting down hard, and I waited, expecting to see blood, but none came; she just kept looking at me, not so much as glancing at the man thrusting away between her legs; then she cried out and began shaking beneath him again; then she forgot she was crying, then forgot him completely and fixed a penetrating gaze on me, then started moaning again and started to get closer; she got so close it felt like she was almost touching me, and I began to feel scared and dizzy. I dreamed about sitting there on the edge of the bed—I dreamed and didn't know how to pull away from her, how to pull her away from me. It was beautiful, like a nightmare of you taking me by force, and frightening, like the thought of us fading away. I didn't tell anyone that day, or even admit it to myself, but I heard her—that woman—calling me, with her eyes and her crimson-painted nails, and that call stayed in my dreams and my nightmares, ringing infinitely like a broken school bell, an infinity that lasted until our apartment on Champollion Street, where it finally stopped, and I didn't miss it.

Baba finished getting dressed and picking up Mama's clothes and turned to me, saw me staring rapt at the screen, so he jabbed a hole in my shoulder with his finger and propelled me out of the room. I'll tell you about the woman, Arwa: she was Asian, she lived inside your average video tape that looked like any other VHS, and Baba took it with him one day when he left the house, and I couldn't rescue it. That night, I was forced to bid her farewell in her bedroom and then sleep by myself on the ground in the main room.

Yes, all these women were in my life before you, maybe as a prelude, or an exercise in patience; I don't know. Now I close my eyes and remember as I, too, sit on the bed, always ready to jump up. I was sad that night, of course, when Baba and his brute strength shoved me out of the bedroom. No one turned off the TV; no one helped lessen my anguish. Who would've, anyway? I didn't see Mama again that night, and I didn't want to think about her; the lady on the tape had taken hold of my mind and set it aflame.

After that, my studies with Mr. Abdallah got better; first thing the next morning, I used a red pen the tutor reserved for corrections to cross out the words "Muhammad Ali" from the box for my name, then came across the answer guide hidden beneath a low table in the main room. It quickly became all mine during those days of isolation: Mama wasn't leaving the bedroom, and Baba only passed through, locking the door behind him, knowing I wouldn't dare come close again. I didn't care; I used the solitude to put my paper on top of the answer sheet and trace out the shapes to get full marks from Mr. Abdallah, all without glancing even once at the locked bedroom door. It got to a point where the man was ready to praise me to the heavens, but there was no one to listen to him. He asked after Mama, raising his voice so she could hear, saying, "I just want to congratulate her on Mariam; I have such great hopes for her!"

I told Baba Mr. Abdallah wanted to talk to him, so he got out some money for him, and Abdallah protested, swearing that he didn't want any extra; he said Mariam would become a doctor when she went to university, then laughed, then asked after Mama. Baba didn't answer, and he wasn't happy; he just put the envelope in Abdallah's shirt pocket, then pressed it tight against his chest to quiet his objections.

Mama had to lie flat for weeks so that Ali, in his new life in the womb, would stick. That was the period in which nothing existed except Mama's sleep, the period during which I was scared she'd forget me, and also feared I would forget. All she did was eat and sleep and get tired out—so tired she couldn't look at me. She stopped working, which Baba agreed to, and he would come back in the afternoons to make food for us, then not eat, just get up again to make long recordings for my grandmother that he would send when he got off work at night, to tell her he was watching and waiting and that the waiting was hard and that he wouldn't put up with it for anyone except Ali, because who else deserved it? He asked her if he would see Ali in his dreams before he was born, then would fall silent for a moment and look at the cassette as though listening for a response, and when she didn't give one, he spoke again. Mama didn't hear any of that, or see him, and I worried she would never come back, and I worried she'd come back with Ali, Ali would come back with her, and I would be stuck with Mr. Abdallah. For hours, in a kind of stupor, she's the only thing I thought of, so many questions I couldn't cheat to get the answers for; when Ali arrived, would Mama tell him "I saw you in my dreams before you were born," just like she'd told me?

One night, I got up when I heard Baba cry out; I stumbled into the bedroom half-awake and bleary-eyed and found them on the bed, Mama with her legs open and him crouched between them. He was trying to stop the flow of blood with his hands, crying as he pressed down, Mama fighting to stay conscious. I didn't know before that night that Baba could cry. He ordered me to hurry and get dressed, and we rushed to the hospital at the end of the street, coloring the ground red, all the way from the door of the apartment to the high metal bed: the black asphalt, the doors, the walls that Mama leaned against on a trip that felt interminable. The scene came to mind again later when I saw the Eid sacrifices scattered through the streets in Cairo; how closely the animals resembled Mama that night. I stayed in the nurses' lounge, with its high ceiling and the neon lightbulbs that burned newborns' eyes; it reminded me of a past I quickly forgot in the young Indian nurse's lap as she held me and rocked me to sleep. I didn't dream about everything that happened; I didn't dream of anything. Ali had died.

> Nine years you've been away, Muhammad. Your father's spent so much time crying for you and not seeing you that his sight is failing. And we didn't see Ali because he died. It was God's will, okay, but Siddiqa—that's it for her. She's not resourceful, and she's not strong, and Mariam is enough for her. Come back to us, Muhammad. You've spent enough time abroad—and all for what? Why are you living there? Saving up money while your son dies in his mother's belly? Your father just says, "It's God's will," and cries. Come back here and marry all the Siddiqas you want. As for the original, we'll let her raise Mariam, and off you go! By law, you get four wives; one of them *has* to give you an Ali. Your father's sight is failing, Muhammad. Really failing. Tonight, all the lights were on at home, and he couldn't find his pills. They were right in front of him! I handed them to him and cried. He's still crying for you. "Muhammad's lost his way," he says. He's even started listening to the Quran on the radio; it's like he's in mourning.

"I know it in my heart," he says. "He's lost his way." So he listens to Surat Yusuf and cries over poor old Yacoub, losing his dreamer son to faraway Egypt and the Pharaoh's court. God knows how sad he really is. Inconsolable. His heart's in a million pieces. For your father, every day's like your funeral, Muhammad. So come back—enough with the time abroad. Forget Ali, and come back here with just Mariam. Take care . . . Bye.

Mama stayed in the hospital for weeks; every time she got a little better, the bleeding would come back, but at least I could see her again. She would complain that the injections were wreaking havoc on her skin, then show me how puffy her hands had gotten from the IV and sedatives and coagulants; she repeated everything the nurses said, and I memorized it all. Mama's face was pale, and nothing made her angry anymore: not if I played or kept quiet, not even if I toyed with her pills. She started calling for me all the time, holding my hand so tightly it hurt, then bursting into tears in front of Baba, in front of the nurses. I would kiss her hand in front of them, too, wading alongside her into the river of her grief. Mariam was her only companion then; I would go home at night with my face puffy from the constant weeping and wailing—like Mama's hand, I thought—and I liked the blueish tinge of my face. At home, I was still the faithful guardian of Mama's sadness, and I prayed to God that he would make the blood go away, that she would be all right again.

She was the most beautiful mother I'd ever seen; it was like reliving our first days together, her tender smile and the nurses presenting me to her after I was born. I told myself I would never love anyone the way I loved her, not even myself; during those days, she told me the story of her prayer and the vow she'd made to Mariam, the chair in the empty room, and the first kiss she'd placed gently on my neck as I slept, blissfully unaware of the world. She talked about my smell, so I tried to describe hers, too, "the most beautiful smell in the whole world, Mama"; accompanied by the sickness and sweat and the metal hospital bed, I could've grasped the scent in my hand, the way someone might grasp a bird. "*You* were like a bird, Mariam; when I saw you, I said to myself, 'Siddiqa, God blessed you with a bird!' My heart was whispering to me that you were like the sparrows—please forgive me, sweetheart." How could I forgive you, Mama, when I was never angry with you? Especially not during that time at the hospital, as you lay there, lacking resources and strength. We would tell each other stories, repeat them a thousand times over, and I was the only thing you still had hope in, our secret that no one else knew about.

Except for Arwa, now, no one knew. For hours, I would stand there contemplating Mama as she slept, lingering on her exposed skin, and I dreamed about covering her with kisses; on the answer pages in my exercise book, I drew a tree spreading its branches to carry a smaller tree, and of course I forgot about Baba at the door, the hospital door, the door of the apartment, at work—where I also pictured him standing at the door—always as if waiting for some piece of news that would make him happy and restore sight to his tired eyes. Baba hadn't cried since the night of the bleeding. He saw people, but he looked through us; I felt that, more than anything, he didn't want to see me.

So I would run away from him and hold on to the tree, but he didn't do anything, didn't chase after me or pick me up; he would walk with me to the house late at night without speaking a word, insisting on holding my hand so I wouldn't get lost, pressing it slightly, and when I looked up at him, he didn't look back at me. I wasn't Baba's companion, or his remaining hope. And I didn't expect to be. I was surprised he didn't just drop my hand; he should've.

Baba left our room at the hospital one day and didn't come back. The next morning, Mr. Abdallah showed up; he knocked on our door, then came in. He smiled when he saw Mama, and his smile widened so much I thought he'd embrace her, which made me suspicious of him. He said he'd looked for us on all the floors of the hospital, but he was lying; he'd only been looking for Mama. Baba was sick, and Mr. Abdallah was taking his place. I don't know how much Baba paid him to play this role, but I was not okay with it, not even a little. He pushed me aside and took my seat and started to feed Mama; he told the nurses he was her brother, and no one checked his story. He raised a cup of water to her lips and smiled at her the way she'd smiled at me before he showed up, and Mama forgot about me and started to recover. Mama betrayed me so many times, Arwa, I lost count. I went back to the nurses' lounge and made friends with the Indian girl, who didn't understand what I was saying but used her halting Arabic to tell me, giving me a kiss, "Mama will be good," then laughed.

I wanted to forget about Mama with her, but it didn't last. One day, Baba came and took us with him to the apartment. When I say "us," I mean me and Mama and Mr. Abdallah, who kept smiling at Mama and getting flustered when she smiled back. As we all climbed the stairs, he carried her bag with as much care as if it were their daughter—his and Mama's.

Mama lay back on the bed, and Baba sat next to her as Abdallah waited for us outside the room (praise God he wasn't allowed farther). When it was time for Baba to say something, anything, before leaving her side, he threw out, "Glad you're better." And without looking, "When you're back up and about, we're going to Egypt." Then he stood and headed for Mr. Abdallah, with me on his heels. He tried to put money in his shirt pocket, as usual, but Abdallah refused this time, insisting he wouldn't take a single riyal. Arwa, I wanted to burn him like a loaf of bread in the oven. Baba gave up and said goodbye, then put the cassette into the tape recorder; he was going to record something for my grandmother. I grabbed the cash from the table and ran after Mr. Abdallah on the stairs, pretending I wanted to thank him, then stuffed the cash into his back pocket unnoticed. I was pretty light-fingered back then; I also stole small toys my father didn't want to buy me. Sorry, Arwa, Mariam used to be a thief.

I locked the door when I got back. I climbed the stairs I'd rushed down shaking with rage, slammed the door closed, and screamed at Baba, "I *hate* Abdallah! He's not coming back here to teach me anything, or I swear to God I'm going to kill myself like Ali did!" Baba didn't answer. My voice had registered on the tape, and he stopped recording, lonely, struggling with himself, eternally starting over.

When I think about all that, it seems only right for there to be an oboe at the end of the road, a mourner to take up my lament and share it with the world. Before you, I never craved anyone or anything the way I craved the oboe; my relationship with it didn't suffer the way my relationship with Mama did, it remained pure because it hadn't been touched or tested; when we met, you and I, and I guessed the instrument in your arms was an oboe, I decided to keep my distance, I didn't take the reed between my lips, it was the only oath I would keep. How did I first come across the oboe, Arwa? I'll tell you. In front of our house was a park that got smaller and smaller the more I grew; it had four sides, each with its own gate, and when I learned a little about geometry, I started calling it the Rectangle Park. It was only green for one month out of the year, yellow and wilting for the rest, with no one to take care of it; the trees reached out unruly, unpruned limbs still heavy with the dust of summer, bending and then falling to the ground, the light wind blowing them away the next day, sending them off without a burial. Even the rain seldom visited the park, coming and going only once in a blue moon. The Rectangle Park meant nothing to anyone except to the Indian and Bangladeshi children who couldn't pay for transportation to the big park downtown and, of course, to me.

I went up the slide and threw my human body onto its steel one that twisted like a snake, scooting down toward the two of them, Baba and Mama, who stood oblivious at the bottom calculating round-trip travel costs. A few little kids climbed up with me and slid down, our only conversation smiles as we took turns, using the gestures and signs all humanity used before language was invented. I barely spoke one language, and they didn't know it, so I couldn't exchange even a word with them, but I can still hear their chatter rising over Mama and Baba's quarrel, him swearing to marry another woman, Mama deciding to move out to escape us both. The sky opened wide for our little arms every day except the rainy ones, when we all ran off with our palms covering our heads, leaving the park all alone, us kids already dreaming of the moment we'd come back to the slide.

Once, I slid down with my eyes closed and arrived at the bottom to the sight of an oboe player. My eyes opened, and that was the beginning.

I saw her during the three days I spent by myself before people finally realized the deceased couple had left a daughter locked in their apartment. I saw her by chance as the channels flipped from one to the next to fill my empty hours, I wasn't scared like the rescuers thought because she was there from Day One and got me through till the end; she was better than the Asian lady and the princesses from Mario, she was more captivating than Mama and all the other women in the world; she was you, Arwa, there before your time, at the beginning. The music came from a group of people all dressed in black and holding their instruments, sitting in an arrangement like a constellation of stars; they didn't care about war or traffic accidents, they were just there, in this vast space I'd never entered, would never enter; it's where you're from, and that's enough for me, one person among many playing on earth. I don't know exactly why I was drawn to her; when the static cleared and I could see her properly, the other players had fallen silent and turned their faces toward her, and I saw the crazy maestro smile and signal to her to start playing. She put the reed between her lips, closed her eyes, and forgot the overturned car in the middle of the road; she breathed into the instrument and continued to blow, and I didn't know a thing about music or symphonies, cannot now even hum the piece she was playing, the piece she's still playing in my heart, but I can say that the camera zoomed so far back I thought I would be swallowed into the frame as I sat there on the ground, lacking resources and strength. My whole body was in my eyes, every tremor mesmerized me, every sigh stifled by a fellow player who watched her and tried not to forget his own instrument, knowing—like me—that in watching her he would lose himself, but not wanting to resist. White as milk, her body bound up in a black dress, the pipe hanging from her lips conveying the melody, she was not just an oboe player; she and the oboe were one body, they called her an oboist because they couldn't find another name. Her black dress made her pale skin look twice as stark; she had short brown hair and swayed violently to the music without ever pausing or looking up to check her cues; she transcended the notes on the page, transcended money, deprivation, the apartment, the dream of return; they tried to stop her so they could play what they'd come to play, gazes toggling between her and the conductor, but they didn't fight it, they let her have her way. I saw the picture flicker, the camera dip to the ground more than once, but my musician didn't stop playing, didn't lift her lips, her nose slightly tilted away from the mouthpiece; then she stood up with her oboe, as though she were directing her music to the heavens, complaining about the world, including her silent listeners, directly to God. I don't remember her plaint or how it ended, but I remember everyone's applause as she fell silent, my applause from the floor in front of the TV, and when my hands began to throb and burn from the force of it, I prayed that my parents wouldn't come back, all I wanted now was to be with her, to kiss this instrument and learn its name, *oboe*, to consecrate its name, and, later, yours, within me.

Then God answered my prayer; my parents didn't come back, and like always, I regretted my prayer, and I missed them. I picked up the telephone receiver to look for Baba at work; at his office, they were transferring all questions to his colleagues' offices, no one skipping a beat. No one seemed to be panicking but me. On the first night, I felt that something bad had happened and that it would be anything but simple to get past it. I lay down in their bed, feeling shame enter and exit my body before it pushed me toward the oboe. At first, I wanted to be her, the oboist, and then, as the night progressed with no explanations, I wanted her to be mine, to sleep with me on the bed as I lay there, alone in the apartment. The next morning, I told myself that the days to come would go by without them, too, and my dreams grew; the musician would fall in love with me and I her, and like a crazy person I started flipping through the TV channels to find her, in the same situation, at another concert or at home or sleeping, just warm and alive and practicing the oboe. I missed her, and the missing and loneliness only got worse. I called Mr. Abdallah and told him they were gone, and he said he'd take care of it. He asked if I had food, water, juice, then asked me to keep the phone line open no matter what.

For a few blessed hours I had no news, and for the first time, I saw what I called my colorful bubbles, spheres that drifted gently down on me from the ceiling and disappeared without a trace. I saw them with eyes both open and closed and would bat at them like a clown as they drifted just out of reach, making me laugh; in the absence of my parents, I entertained myself with the bubbles, with the oboist; the world gave of itself to me lavishly, as if compensating for something I was afraid to ask about. I imitated her in every corner of our apartment to help suppress my anxiety at night, and I played the oboe, breathing out melodies that flowed from my tongue, my palm, my clothes, grateful to God because this was a sign of her dissolving into me. Then the phone rang, Arwa, and I said, "Hello?" And Mr. Abdallah's voice came down the line, "Do you have a key to the door?" When I said no, he got angry for the first time and said, "How could they leave you without a key, what if there was a fire?" He suggested breaking down the door, and I laughed sarcastically. "Did you forget it's metal?"

Everyone went looking for them—Baba's colleagues at work, his bosses, even his work sponsor—the search lasted two days, during which time the police got involved and came to the apartment. They talked to me from the other side of the door, said they would use a blowtorch to get through the metal, but I refused and told them I was a girl alone in the apartment and I wouldn't okay that, the sound of the tools scared me, and I knew I couldn't bear it, and then I didn't know where I would *go* if the door was opened. I wanted to live like I was just fine, patiently, comforted; the oboist didn't leave my side for a second, she played with the bubbles alongside me, and they helped us to play her instrument, too; the policemen listened and left, leaving a guard at the door who would stay until they were found. Then they received the news, and they took the two bodies to al-Yamama Hospital—the place I was born, remember?

Mama died.

I heard the news from Mr. Abdallah, as he hit his head against the wall opposite the door. He vomited on the stairs, pacing up and down them, disoriented, not sure what to do other than weep and wail, I saw it all—heard it—from behind the door, locked into the apartment. He was sad and didn't think to justify the reasons behind it, but I knew; like the camera on the day of the concert, I walked through the apartment tripping, falling on my face more than once. After all the joy, the bubbles disappeared, and the oboist evaporated. I felt like I was suffocating under that low ceiling with its yellow light bulb, and I started screaming and banging on the door, just wanting to breathe. Arwa, I couldn't believe Mama was gone for good.

I slept for days, and then the blinding whiteness of hospitals again began to burn my eyes, my heart sank every time I woke up and didn't find her there beside me, only the nurses who looked at me with such deep pity that they slipped their needles into my arms gingerly, a gentle press of fingertips. I cried, not knowing who I would live with now, and Mr. Abdallah came and took my hand in his and kissed it because I was the only thing left of my wonderful mother, and without thinking about it I told him, "Don't ever forget her," and bowed my head in mourning. His beard trembled like a leaf, holding on weakly against the wind, and he told me how they'd found the key in Baba's pocket and how his hand was clenched around it, as if he were showing the person who would inspect his body how to find me. "Baba loves you so much, Mariam." That was Mr. Abdallah's opinion of his rival, Arwa.

I could've gone to the morgue to see them one last time, but I was afraid, and Abdallah was afraid for me. Instead, we sat on the wheelchairs in the white corridor, and he gave me an idea about what would happen next. He told me he wouldn't leave me until I got to Egypt and that my grandmother would take me in, that before I left they would pay me the wrongful death damages they owed me, so much money I would never need to take charity from anyone. Mama and Baba had dreamed of having that kind of money, Arwa.

"They'll visit you in your dreams, especially Mama, any time you need her. Everyone in Egypt will love you because you're all that's left of them. Study hard in school, no cheating, remember you'll die someday, too, and you'll see them again in that other world." "Aren't you coming back with me to Egypt, Abdallah?" "It's not time for me yet. Take care of yourself until your loved ones come to take care of you. While you're on the plane up above the clouds, ask God for them, and he'll answer." "What if I want to stay at the apartment, for one last night?" "There's no point. You'll just disturb the dead. Come on, the plane's waiting, I'll take care of everything; come on, don't dawdle. . ."

I was afraid of takeoff, but unlike the children around me, I put on a rare brave face and didn't cry. I drank juice and slept, then awoke to see that I was swimming through a sea of dazzling clouds, aloft in the body of a giant ship with wings, called a plane. I screamed with the little kids when we hit turbulence, and I clapped with the others when we landed, finally, on Egyptian soil, the country of Muhammad Ali, and my country. All the family came in from Upper Egypt, from the Sa'id, and stood waiting to receive me; they wore black as a symbol of new mourning, a sign of my kinship with them, but didn't hold any musical instruments. The women wailed and the men wept as they took my bag from me; my grandmother hugged me, she looked like Baba but with larger streaks of white hair; she hugged me and said, "God help us!" and then we went outside and I saw the sky and thought, I want to die and be buried here. This was the new world, Arwa, and nothing in it reminded me of the old one. Looking back now, I think it helped me forget: except for the days I had nightmares filled with ghosts, or when I was sick or conflicted, I actually forgot the two of them. This is all I remember of them, Arwa, all I remember about myself. And now . . . do you know, my love, who I am now?

2

I didn't have time to stress over some impending doom; Arwa beckoned before I'd even gotten a grip on myself, and I went straight to her. The first time, we met by the High Court of Justice. The day was shaping up to be just another day when my phone lit up with an unknown number from Europe—probably a misdial, and I'd be stuck on the line for ages listening to apologies and excuses. But I had some time to spare, so I said, "Hello?" And someone, her voice sweet, said, "Hi Mariam, it's Arwa." Surely, God, You remember with me, remember the spit I swallowed and almost choked on. "Yes! Yes." "I'd like to meet up with you, Mariam," and I repeated myself, "Yes," nothing else. I agreed to everything before you spoke, before we'd even specified the time or place and without thinking about the revolution. I went to get ready and, for hours, afternoon to early evening, paced in front of the mirror, practicing my smile and trying to remember how you looked in the metro.

Only You could see me gasping for breath as I rode the microbus to Abdul Monim Riad Square, my pulse waxing and waning, inexorably ticking like the grandfather clock in the sitting room that clanged madly with each new hour that arrived. What exactly was I expecting of Arwa? I don't know. Stepping off the bus into the crowd, I told myself that even if I missed our appointment, her promise to meet me was all I needed to be happy; I stumbled as I made my way from sidewalk to sidewalk until I turned onto Champollion Street and my heart clenched again because, unless I was remembering wrong, that's where she'd told me she lived. I continued along, past poor souls living in fear of a moment that would betray them, in fear of gunfire or random arrests, even of fleeing demonstrators who might accidentally trample them. I walked with my eyes straight ahead, skirting closed shops and their faded signs. I climbed up and down over piles of stones that someone was using for who knows what. I started taking mental pictures and engraving them onto my memory so I would never forget: this is how Champollion looked that day.

I put out my hand when I was still a few feet away from her; she was standing next to a lamppost that hadn't flicked on yet, looking toward the other street, the one I wasn't coming from, as if she weren't waiting for me. As I came closer, I raised my voice as much as I could, "Hi! How are you?" and she turned, and her smile widened. She was different even than in the metro, her arms crossed over her chest, as if she were hiding something, and she was wearing all black—shirt, pants, and clogs, in spite of the frigid weather, which gave me a start for some reason. This was another Arwa, her shoulders broader than a musician's, more like a tennis or squash player's, she shifted from reality to fantasy and reality to reality. One thing stayed, another thing shifted;

she said, "Hi Mariam, I was worried you got held up." "No, I promised I'd be here."

"I figured you were still upset." Then she laughed, covering her mouth.

At that moment, I felt sure it was all in my head; none of this was actually happening. She took my hand and pulled me toward Champollion Street. I couldn't hold her hand the way I'd wanted to, but I didn't take mine back. I just wanted to be led, to follow behind her to a spot I guessed at but couldn't know. "Do you want to go to my place on Champollion or find someplace closer?" "I'm sick of being inside—but where's your oboe?" She was looking at me, forcing me to maintain eye contact as she spoke, guiding me to keep me from tripping, to steer me around broken pavement and the few motorcycles that appeared out of nowhere and zoomed past as if driven by the ghosts of those who'd died on that spot. You know she kept me on the inside of the sidewalk, and didn't squeeze my hand. "It all happened so fast," she was saying. "It only took a couple of hours to decide to come, and a couple more hours to be on my way." "You mean to come to Egypt?" "Yeah, I have German nationality; I renounced my Egyptian." She didn't seem to like looking at me now, concentrated on the potholes and the end of the dark street, she was shy. I wanted to grab her other hand.

"Is there a difference?" "Honestly, everything's different. Would you rather just walk around a little instead of being inside or going to a coffee shop?" "Maybe . . ." I knew I would be sick of the cold soon. I was hiding my chest, too, pulling my too-small jacket tight around me.

"Just not near the demonstrations." "'Demonstrations'? Is that what you're calling them? People are dying over there." For a second, I thought she was talking about Munich, but she tilted her head in the direction of the Talaat Harb statue, and I realized she meant the American University.

A few mechanics still had their garage doors open but were getting ready to close; night had settled over the world. "You come here a lot?" "Downtown, yes, but Champollion, no." "Do you wanna eat some koshary at Abou Tarek's?" I couldn't keep from laughing at the thought of this German woman eating koshary, and I kept laughing as she stared at me nonplussed, without asking why. Then her eyes gleamed and she raised her eyebrows at me as if to ask, *Okay, and?* I was embarrassed and turned my feet automatically in the direction of the restaurant. It was dark, its only light fixture, inside, a simple one.

"Do you know what happened when you called earlier?" "What?" "I was sitting on the ground watching TV with my grandfather, who lost his eyesight ages ago, and he said he saw the girl, too, plain as day, just like we did." "What girl?" We'd left Abou Tarek's and started walking again in the darkness. "The girl they stripped naked." "I heard about that." "Good." We stopped abruptly to let a large car pass. "What's good?" "I mean, it's good you didn't see it." She wasn't satisfied with my answer, though: "You know what I thought when I first heard about that girl? I thought I should go play my oboe naked in front of the Central Security vehicles."

This time, she was walking a step ahead of me, without turning around, and I dawdled a little to get her attention, so she paused for me but still wouldn't look at me; I was on her left, so she turned her head to the right and said, "My burden's a lot for you to carry, Mariam." The sudden entrance into our story—that marker of our entrance into it—surprised me; I've loved beginnings since my days in Mama's womb and thought I would never love anyone but her—but I loved frankness, too, more than anything. I considered what she'd said: "A lot for who?" Arwa was nervous about something, something I couldn't yet name. "Here's my place." She gestured to a building on the corner where El Tak'eeba Café stood, a landmark for later, and then pointed up: "It's on the fourth floor of that super old building. If you ever want to visit . . ."

Then, without another word, she decided to take me back to Abdul Monim Riad Square. "Want me to walk you to the microbus stop?" I objected as the voice inside me, the one saying I didn't want to leave, grew louder. We stopped and faced each other at the security barrier before crossing the street; she was smiling again, she looked away to hide the smile, as if all this torture had never happened.

"Mariam, how old are you?" "Twenty-four springs, summers, autumns, and winters." "A poet, too, are you?" Her hand moved back to cover her mouth. "Well, *I've* seen thirty-four autumns, winters, and summers, and you remind me of the people I've loved. You have the same scent, the same laugh. But you're young." I plucked up my courage and told her I wanted to hear about the people she'd loved and that I didn't want to go home; I grabbed her hand and walked, dragging her back toward

Champollion Street. "You're coming back with me, and I'm not going to leave." Arwa let me pull her along, her appreciation leaping from her eyes and her dull, compact smile, as though this was all she'd wanted from the start.

"You're familiar with hell, Mariam?" Mariam swallowed hard—I wanted to say I didn't like the topic. "Yes, Arwa. I'm familiar." "What is hell, Mariam?" I didn't stop to think about it; I said that hell was the opposite of the time we were living in. It was as if the angel had landed on my head and whispered the answer in my ear. "Okay, Marioum, let's say *I* am hell, and that hell is burning and freezing and running and playing music, most of it out of tune—do you think you'd be happy there?" That time you beat me to the poetry, Arwa.

I would still agree to enter hell, Angel, as long as Arwa was with me.

I decided we would walk back to her place so she wouldn't have any way out; I would climb the stairs with her to the fourth floor, and I got myself ready to yell, "What, I can't come in?" if she declined to invite me, but her hand fell from mine as I waged my own inner battle. That only fanned the flames of my determination; I would pull her by her arm, by her belt loops, but she was laughing, and that's what I saw when I turned abruptly—I saw her laughing, finally, and I lost sight of myself in the scene. She slipped from one burst of laughter to the next in waves, beginning, cresting, ending. She stared at me for a few seconds each time before she began laughing again. I don't know how long Arwa kept laughing, or how many times she bent over double or clutched her chest, as if the laughter were splitting it.

"Your cheeks are all red." In all my life, I'd never made anyone laugh as hard as I made Arwa laugh, and I didn't want the show to end. She looked back at me, happy, but no longer laughing, "Marioum, you're insane," and she smiled before something made that happiness dissipate, and her expression dulled again. "Call me. Go home, think a bit, and call me." Home. I'd forgotten about home, and that old life, how was I supposed to go back—how? She walked with me to the spot where I was meant to cross the street, and I pouted to show her I was upset, ravished her with my eyes as she left, already barely aware of my presence. She walked toward the Abdul Monim Riad statue with a look on her face I didn't understand. All I could think about was touching her hand one last time, that her touch would dispel "home," but I was too afraid to reach for it.

Of course You didn't want all that to happen. She left me to cross the street alone, and I was heartsick because she didn't embrace me the way people casually embrace every day in Cairo. I was so upset that I couldn't turn back and look for her. Was she still watching as I crossed over like an animal, hungry and distraught, knowing there was no food on the other side? Or was she halfway back to her apartment on Champollion by now? What would make me sadder, her not taking me home or that she had laughed so much with me and then abandoned me?

When the microbus passed that spot on its way back through, I gave myself permission to look at the place where we'd parted ways, and of course she wasn't there. I leaned my head against the plastic windowpane, which no longer opened because its handles had been removed, looked at the ceiling of the bus and told You, *Fine*, told her, *Fine*. I wanted to sleep, and from the apartment door I aimed immediately for my room to avoid my grandmother. No such luck. When I came in, she was in the sitting room with two of our neighbors, crying, her head wrapped in a red scarf with a single yellow rose on it. The women sat on either side of her, trying to comfort her and reciting the Quran; this same old movie was playing again, for the millionth time. I knew there would be no peace tonight, no restful sleep; the ghosts were coming, and they would hunt me all the way to the threshold of my dreams.

I was closing the door behind me when I heard her say, "Mariam is all I have left of Muhammad." Her words made the women cry, and I didn't feel like the Mariam she was talking about, even though she was looking straight at me; nothing would change even if I did feel that way. How could Arwa have come back to my apartment when you're in it, too, Sitti? I wanted to ask her that but didn't have a chance because one of the women came and buried my face in her bosom, enveloping me against my will in the scent of onions and incense and sweat. "Oh, Mariam, you're all your grandmother has left; the streets are so dangerous now—don't go out anymore." I said okay, extracting myself from her embrace and looking back at my grandmother. I was hungry, so I asked her if there was anything to eat; the question made her eyebrows shoot up and her eyes bulge, and she responded through clenched teeth: "Well, I made fish, but then the locusts descended." She was determined to play out her role in this film, and I was exhausted, so

I took up the line again to give her an opening. "The locusts ate all the fish?" She said they'd left me a piece on the stove, and I smiled: what generous locusts.

I looked like a monkey eating off the stove, didn't I? Like I was trying to steal a banana from the jungle as my tribe mourned my father's death hundreds of years ago, even though they're the ones who killed him. I didn't deserve someone like Arwa to fall in love with me: how could a human love a monkey? I finally admitted it for the first time as I ate with my hands, bits of food falling from my mouth, I admitted it as I got ready for the next scene in my grandmother's drama, the part where she screamed and collapsed, then sobbed more quietly; everything I did had to be quick, including pining after Arwa. It was bad enough that I couldn't avoid the ending, where Sitti would stand on the balcony looking down and admonish God, "He was my only son," until all the windows opened and people looked out at the woman who'd gone mad when her son died abroad.

They believed her even though they knew Muhammad wasn't her only son, that in fact four other men called her Mama every morning and evening as the door swung shut behind them. They were sorry for her, understanding that she hadn't really gone mad, that she was good at everything, even dying of sadness, her eyes bulging beneath sleepless eyelids. You know what she means when she looks down at the ground and talks to You; she addresses, mocks, and challenges You, then asks for forgiveness and divine compensation, and You won't punish her, as if she and no one else sees You there, as if her loss gives her a depth of vision no one else in Cairo has. Not once have I asked why she sees You down there. Not once did I voice my thought that devils that are supposed to live underground . . . not the Lord of the Heavens.

Really, how could Arwa have come home with me?

It was pointless even to consider it. She would've thought I was like my grandmother; sometimes I thought so, too, that I looked like her in some way I couldn't quite put my finger on. Arwa would've run away from me, run away and never come back. *Enough*, I thought, and I made myself a cup of warm milk and cut a path to my grandfather's room. When he whispered I was late, I apologized loudly so he could hear. I swore not to do it again, so I wouldn't make him any sadder, and I meant it—I didn't expect what was to come. I closed my bedroom door, climbed into bed with my phone, and pulled the covers over me, switching on the radio function. What sadness were you masking, Arwa? Why did you fall into my life if you were going to turn to dust so quickly? I congratulated myself as I fell asleep, persuaded I would forget, just as I had forgotten everything before.

When your text message first pinged, Mariam, I thought you'd replied faster than you should've, that you were young and wanted to experiment, wanted to know. I thought about just ignoring the whole thing and stayed up all night wavering between the bed and the door. In the end, I asked myself what could possibly happen that hadn't already? I called you and told you to come over; if a blind man gets smacked in the eye, what's he lost anyway—do people still say that, Mariam? All right, Arwa, you got rid of the millstone round your neck, and now you're spitting jokes. Old jokes that made it to Europe late. I don't know what might happen, I don't even know what happened in the past, but you keeping me at arms' length is something else, it's humiliating—I'm not that young. *Well, you're younger than you think; we're ten years apart, you're light years younger than me, and I can leave at any time, but you . . . where would you go?*

In my message, I wrote to you, "Take me to hell, Arwa," so do you think all that matters to me? I looked up your German number without even knowing if I could send my little poem with the phone plan I was on; it was the very last straw, did you want me to beg you? *Mariam, don't think that; I'm sorry, so sorry, Mariam, and sad. Knowledge is bitter.* What did that knowledge do to you, Arwa? Did it take away your sadness? *No one can take away sadness; we've just learned to live with it.* I'm sad, too, Arwa—fine, not right now, but I swear sadness is present in me. Maybe it can hear me talking to you; maybe, Arwa, you can set it free. Who knows?

"What is it you want to happen between us?"

Arwa, I swear you were trying to brush me off. "Nothing. I don't want anything to happen; I'm leaving." I jumped up and opened the door; I would go down those stairs and never come back to this building as long as I lived, I wouldn't pass by it, I wouldn't remember anyone who even *looked* like you—and then I felt two hands on my shoulders. The gentle touch was coming from behind and refracting in two directions with me at the center, like light in a pane of glass. We were in the hallway, blocking the corridor. At that moment, I looked down, imagining the height of the building under my feet, imagining the hole I would fall into, because I would fall, and I wouldn't stop myself. "I want you." We went inside, the door closed behind us, and for the first time in years, I felt like crying.

First I cried when the doorman asked me whose apartment I was visiting and then, when I said "Arwa's," pursed his lips and asked disapprovingly, "Arwa who? Sara's daughter?" My eyes grew moist when I said yes, even though I didn't know who this Sara was. Just another secret of yours, right? Right. You can escape any time, but I no longer have the ability to go back where I came from. With each step I took to get here, the thing I kept pushing from my mind was the question, *Who do* you *think I am?* All I had to do was reach the fourth floor, knock on your door and no one else's, see your face and no one else's. And whoever you thought I was, I was so much more ridiculous. Then I heard the creaking of the stiff wooden door and an apology—mine: "I'm sorry I'm so late." "Don't worry about it, Mariam, welcome, come in."

I never thought this was how it would be when I finally got here. I stepped back in confusion, then forward again, and you kissed me in greeting. I entered the apartment despite the dim light that didn't seem right for guests, thought about taking my shoes off and walking barefoot, but on what?—even the floors were bare. It took less than a minute for me to understand that everything in this space was protected against outsiders, and I was just one more outsider. The relics of the old living room were a faded olive green that had transformed since you left Egypt, making it impossible, now, to tell their original color, and only the overstuffed red chair reassured me. To my admiring eyes, it looked like a throne that didn't match its palace, and maybe the room would change to match. It looked like a small bed, the kind of cradle where children sleep in the movies, or potentially a bed for grown-ups, if we threw those pillows on the floor—and when did this thing arrive if you only got to Cairo a few days ago? But still, like the stranger, the guest I was, I ignored it and sat on the sofa, heard it groan as I settled in. I sat facing you as you held inside you words you avoided saying, looked at me, folded your arms over your chest, looked away, and finally asked, "Would you take some coffee?"

"I'd love some." The apartment was shaped like a triangle, its base made up of two rooms. The one at the far end resembled a brightly lit studio, its window open to the bustle of the café and its customers below, and closer to me was the dark bedroom, its door ajar, inviting. I was in the living room, perched at the top of the triangle, waving to those who'd undoubtedly passed through here. When you came back, you'd pulled yourself together, that much was clear from the tone of your voice, from the slight flutter of your eyelids as you held out a cup and said, "Here," as if it were the last time you'd pronounce that word in this context, and I started to feel my eyes aching in the half-light. The silence was no longer comforting to me, and your gaze on me made the text I'd sent you echo in the stillness, *Take me to hell, Arwa*, like a condemnation, and I blushed, I was embarrassed, of course I was, because what kind of idiot walks right into a torture chamber, and you began to murmur, stopped, then demanded an explanation for why I'd come.

I didn't want an explanation; you misunderstood me. If I had, why would I keep smiling at you, encouraging you to smile as you spoke? Well, all I can say is that *I* was smiling just to keep from crying, that's all, so you wouldn't say anything more hurtful. Why did you hide yourself from me, Arwa? I thought I'd be fine no matter what, that I'd forget you; I looked at the door and told myself I would get up to go, and you saw that in my eyes, so you spoke, but instead of saying anything, anything at all, you went back to that question: "Why did you text me?" Your eyes were wide, questioning, and it was unbearable, but I bore it.

I had jerked awake. Not because of the nightmare—I always have nightmares, don't worry about that. I couldn't tell you the key points or any specifics, but it had nothing to do with you, at least not directly. But I woke up around dawn with my heart racing. I got out of bed and opened the window, trying to guess what time it was; the sky was still dark. You know what goes through your mind when you wake up like that, how you feel like you need to tell someone you're all right, maybe someone in particular, maybe anyone? Believe me, though, I didn't have time to think about my wording: the day was fighting to break, but fighting against what, I didn't know. I found myself holding my phone and saying aloud, "Take me to hell, Arwa." Maybe it was the traces of my dream and nothing more; maybe I don't have an explanation.

Tripping over my words, I told her everything I knew, to make my words believable; *I* wanted to know what made me write that, too. Arwa leaned her cheek against one hand, rested her other palm on her thigh, and as I spoke, she lifted her head, her body humming almost imperceptibly as she stared at me but didn't see me; instead, she saw me sleeping in my bed that night, saw my panic and experienced my visions, I had to confess everything, maybe I'd heard the sentence I wrote to her in my dreams. I lost her, like someone wandering in one street and looking for another; my only hope was to stay lost, to keep trying in all this madness to meet her on some street corner.

"I mean, I really wanted to answer your question; you told me to think about it and let you know, so maybe I thought about it while I was sleeping, kind of. But I was conscious when I wrote to you; I swear I meant to do it. But whatever—what did you think when you got the text? Thanks for the coffee, by the way, really."

When your text message first pinged, Mariam, I thought you'd replied faster than you should've, that you were young and wanted to experiment, wanted to know, I thought about just ignoring the whole thing and stayed up all night wavering between the bed and the door. In the end, I asked myself what could possibly happen that hadn't already? I called you and told you to come over; if a blind man gets smacked in the eye, what's he lost anyway—do people still say that, Mariam? All right, Arwa, you got rid of the millstone round your neck, and now you're spitting jokes. Old jokes that made it to Europe late. I don't know what might happen, I don't even know what happened in the past, but you keeping me at arms' length is something else, it's humiliating—I'm not that young. *Well, you're younger than you think; we're ten years apart, you're light years younger than me, and I can leave at any time, but you . . . where would you go?*

In my message, I wrote to you, "Take me to hell, Arwa," so do you think all that matters to me? I looked up your German number without even knowing if I could send my little poem with the phone plan I was on; it was the very last straw, did you want me to beg you? *Mariam, don't think that; I'm sorry, so sorry, Mariam, and sad. Knowledge is bitter.* What did that knowledge do to you, Arwa? Did it take away your sadness? *No one can take away sadness; we've just learned to live with it.* I'm sad, too, Arwa—fine, not right now, but I swear sadness is present in me. Maybe it can hear me talking to you; maybe, Arwa, you can set it free. Who knows?

"What is it you want to happen between us?"

Arwa, I swear you were trying to brush me off. "Nothing. I don't want anything to happen; I'm leaving." I jumped up and opened the door; I would go down those stairs and never come back to this building as long as I lived, I wouldn't pass by it, I wouldn't remember anyone who even *looked* like you—and then I felt two hands on my shoulders. The gentle touch was coming from behind and refracting in two directions with me at the center, like light in a pane of glass. We were in the hallway, blocking the corridor. At that moment, I looked down, imagining the height of the building under my feet, imagining the hole I would fall into, because I would fall, and I wouldn't stop myself. "I want you." We went inside, the door closed behind us, and for the first time in years, I felt like crying.

We didn't have time to cry, or we chose to cry in our own way. I went inside, and when I turned around, I found my nose between her lips. I was slower, so I didn't quite realize what was happening, but it was wonderful, the movement shook me, the knowledge that she was now kissing my nose shook me; it shook me to follow the scene in detail. She took my nose into her mouth, and when I relaxed into stillness, she began to tickle the peach fuzz on the outer edges of my nostrils with the tip of her tongue, dazing me, easing my fear of continuing; she tried to enter into me along with my breath, and I closed my eyes and surrendered to her in the darkness; she came and went, ebbing and flowing against my skin, never pushing me too far and never stopping, finally seeming to tire of it and venturing a bite that even a child could handle, as though warning me that she could envelop my entire nose with her mouth but consoling me that she wouldn't.

She stopped when she felt I couldn't take anymore, in spite of myself; if it were up to me, I'd take the nose off my face and give it to her as a gift, or let her write on it with her tongue forever, safe in the knowledge that nothing so prosaic could separate us, but I needed oxygen. I was shaken again when I opened my eyes and saw the fire in her features, the ruddiness of her face, the nose I hadn't kissed, the lips, and her eyes, which were pinkish and glowing like a wolf's, maybe like a wolf's. She was mostly still, but her breath came in gasps, and her green eyes sparkled, an invitation to something, though I didn't yet know what. I asked, nervously, "What's wrong?" and lifted my hand to hide my eyes, as though she'd slapped me, not kissed me. Even that imagined slap was worthwhile, coming from her. She grasped my index finger, which I held suspended in midair like someone stumbling upon a thought after a night of insomnia; she grasped it and smiled, squeezed and beamed even more, spoke in a voice that was new to my ears then and became familiar later, more so with each time we made love: "You said you decided; do you regret it yet?" No, I didn't regret it. "Okay, sit." I obeyed, and as I sat back down, I felt that I was turning into the camera the day of the oboist's concert, zooming in at the same time as I pulled back, and finally falling to the ground. I was dizzy and afraid to say my world was spinning. My lack of experience was embarrassing: what effect had the kiss had on her? The very slight trembling, or just the echo of my own trembling, the flush that wasn't just flowering over her face or chest but even the exposed parts of her arms and fingers, and when I lowered my eyes to the ground to hide my gaze, I glimpsed her feet in their clogs, and all poetry aside, they were like two wild roses in an expensive florist's shop in spring, a spring like Cairo had never seen. She was still standing there next to the door, the location of the kiss, the question, the plea, trying to organize the mixture of feelings my nose provoked, and, with her eyes, she said, *What?* and I answered with the first thing that came to mind: "You can't be human." Her pupils jumped to my index finger as I extended it unthinkingly for the tenth time; the color on Arwa's skin was creeping onto my hand, even from a distance, and I yelped as I watched it progress: "You're not human, Arwa, you're a contagion!" And, of course, she burst out laughing.

Her laughter took from me everything it needed to, and we dissolved together into mirth, relaxing. We were laughing, so we had to be okay. She said, "You must be thirsty" and went into the kitchen. I leaned back into the couch, feeling my wetness against my clothing; if

I moved too abruptly, it would reach my pants, then soak through onto the fabric of the couch, and nothing Arwa could do would clean it away, however much she tried. It was the first time in my life I'd been this wet, the first time my scent had reached the outside world, had reached my own nose, and I realized now that I had a scent, like every other human.

Just so you know, Arwa. The sudden scandal between my legs, I had to find a way to put off telling you the truth until it dried—at least a little. I knew you were patient about these things, and they were all new to me. When you came back with a plastic water bottle in one hand and a glass in the other, I told myself that the redness spreading over your body, as intense as ever, was your own scandal; you'd had to hide for a moment, like me, until you were yourself again. You smiled a new smile this time; I wasn't a guest anymore, Arwa. Finally, you turned on the light and talked for a long time, but not a word penetrated my mind; do you remember how you perched on the edge of your seat? With your arms, your fingers, your fingernails, you sketched every phrase, emphasized every word, as if I were deaf. The moment we kissed, you entered into my bloodstream like a fever. Speak, and my words will fall away. I saw myself as a rabbit applauding the magician who'd hidden me in his hat with the same fervor as the audience; all logic, you laid out the evolution of your attitude toward me before I'd arrived . . . but, Arwa, what role does logic play in this?

You were afraid for me, you said, you weren't sure this was what I really wanted, you weren't some plaything in a toy store to try out—at this point, I laughed aloud, laughter that was reproachful, resentful, or foolish, I couldn't tell—and changing my "lifestyle" like this wouldn't be easy, especially here: forget taking Mariam to hell; it would bring hell straight to Mariam. "Really, Arwa? Can it get more like hell than this? I'm afraid to watch TV and die of shock, and any day now I could suffocate to death in the metro; all they have to do is tear gas the protestors as I pass the Sadat stop. You have no idea how insignificant my life is." "I'm sorry, Mariam, I'm sorry." You broke into the misery I was describing, then looked at me seriously, questioningly. "But none of that matters to you just now. Right?" Instead of asking what I now realized I'd come all this way for, I started shaking like an epileptic. I could already confirm my answer was yes; it was the only thing in my life I was sure of.

"Would you play for me?"

That day in the metro, several things kept me from listening to you—you most of all. I wish I could see you again now for the first time; if there were a metro station in this old building and we sat now as we did then, I wouldn't mind at all; things have changed so much. "I'll play for you, but will you ask me first?" "Ask what?" "Ask me who I am, and tell me about you." I exhaled and pulled away. "It's always the same story . . ." She looked taken aback: "Why do I feel like I'm bothering you?" The story about my primary and secondary schooling, my friends and the number of siblings I have, what Baba does, Mama does, every answer a new nothing added to the world. No milestones or accomplishments worth mentioning, not a single struggle similar to yours. What was enticing about my life, Arwa?

A touch on the arm I had resting on the wooden armrest made me less distressed to be so boring, made me try to respond. I got lost in the streets; if you considered getting lost an accomplishment, I would ride the metro to the end of the line, staring into people's eyes as they stared back at me, and then we'd all get on with our lives. I pretended I had a life like theirs to get on with. I had my grandmother and grandfather, a room to myself, and an inheritance from my parents that would last the rest of my life. Classmates and friends I'd gathered during each academic year I failed at university, meaning that our bond never lasted long or officially ended. One-line poems I didn't know how to complete, an extensive past, and sick notes dating back to age ten that I'd filed away carefully, along with myriad prescriptions, my name scribbled in the blanks next to "Patient."

But honestly, all this was nothing, Arwa. "Mariam" was nothing and nobody. "Will you kick me out now because I'm here begging you for a life?"

"What, because Arwa's a princess? I'm the one begging *you* for a life, Mariam. I'm begging at the feet of a born poet, from a long line of poets; there's no life richer than one with you. Sure, I'll play for you, but do you want to ask me for my story first?"

"No, play for me first."

The first time I saw the oboe inside your house was the prelude to the sweetest days the world has ever seen. The musical instrument I'd dreamed about for years seemed ordinary in your hands, and to keep my oath that I'd never touch it myself, I said, "Play anything you like." In the end, I only knew the sounds of classical music, not the big names or their classifications. "Sometimes I mess around with stuff I compose myself, but you might not like it." "Just play—it doesn't matter if it's upbeat or slow, or even out of tune; it would be beautiful then, too, coming from you. As long as the wailing doesn't end up annoying the doorman so much that he curses Ms. Sara."

The image in my mind developed like this: you walked toward the studio that wasn't really a studio, just another room leading inside, after springing lightly to your feet and spinning in space, looking for the oboe case, your hand on your forehead as if that might help you find it quicker. You signaled to me to follow you, and I obeyed even before you signaled. You crossed your legs and plopped to the ground, taking the position of the famous Egyptian scribe in pharaonic sculpture. I still remember the effort on your face as you blew forcefully into the double reed; your fingers touching the keys as the instrument rang out like a bell, or a scream; your resistance to the scream; and the possibility inherent in your absence as you played, trying to keep me close. Did you compose all this, Arwa? Why didn't you tell me about it that day in the metro? A hand motioned for me to sit on the floor, and I collapsed beside you, upset without knowing why.

But you moved, pressing your shoulder against mine, and I could feel your yearning. I found myself getting wetter and wetter, abnormally so, like someone tumbling from a waterfall into a river that hasn't yet reached up to catch them. How could I make it stop? I sighed because you were going to find out, from the scent if nothing else, so I'd better go ahead and tell you. I raised a finger to stop your playing, and you raised your eyebrows. I turned my finger down, pointing at my lap, not knowing how to explain. "I'm . . . when you touch me, my soul is . . . drowning, Arwa. Is that normal?" Your laughter was enough to fill an entire country, making you drop your oboe and flush again before you finally regained your composure and stroked my thigh and told me it was the most normal thing in the world.

You were diaphanous, pellucid through to the bone. When you got up, my heart sank deeper into my chest. You stood in front of the window, which was open to the night outside, and I realized you were about to take off your shirt. This was it, and I wasn't ready. I hugged my arms to my chest, the feeling of cold growing as you undid your buttons one after the other, letting the wind blown in by the street pass over you and press against your bra. I tried to speak and failed because your gaze was steady, even as it moved between me and the shirt. As though you were an actress in a movie you once starred in, you tossed the shirt onto the ground a few feet from me; it would've made sense for me to crawl toward it, but I was paralyzed. I began to tremble, knowing that what had just happened would be repeated with everything you were wearing.

Clad in your thin bra, you unbuttoned your black pants just as slowly, forcing me to look as I steeled myself not to run away. The plastic button clicked as it hit the floor next to the shirt, and your long legs glimmered like a triangle spreading out wide from its vertex, which was clothed in a light scrap of yellow. I wasn't just wet now, I was flooding—*enough, Arwa, please*. "Get up, Mariam." A hand extended, beckoning me to the window. Lightheaded, I got up, and hoped that I would fall and the scene would end, but that didn't happen. I crossed my arms, obeyed you, and came closer. I would say the first thing that came to mind, "You're gorgeous, Arwa." You didn't laugh, not even at my bumbling, as I'd thought you would. "I'm not gorgeous, Mariam. I love you." You said it impatiently, as though it were a universal truth and you were tired of me not knowing. I obeyed you and came closer when you said, "Touch me. Ask me."

You raised your arms high, the way protesters raise their arms to the police, then brought them down, taking off your bra in a sudden, acrobatic movement. I didn't know what to expect, and that flustered me, Arwa, so much that I wanted to burst into tears and leave. You rested one arm on my shoulder and pulled off the last scrap of fabric with the other, revealing a smattering of light-colored hair trying to cover up the source. No one would've stopped you at this point, right? Of course not. "Ask me, Mariam. Ask me." "I'm scared." "Give me your hand, and ask." "How, Arwa?"

"Do you want to know me? Answer me, do you want to know who Arwa is?" "Yes." So Arwa told me. "I start here." The first place I felt the electric shock was in my hand, my hand on your heart, the fear receding as I rested my palm on the scarlet, pulsing flesh. You were quiet until that feeling reached me, then began your recitation: "This is where I found the strength to leave Egypt, and the strength to come back. And this . . ." You moved my hand to your belly. "This is where you were supposed to begin, or where I did"—which stomach was yours, Arwa? "Here—don't be scared, Mariam—I can pull you into my womb and run away with you, so far and fast that no one can reach you." With my senses this heightened, I could run through all of Germany and all of Egypt ablaze, and my fire would consume the entire planet. "You're all red." "I am . . . And here," my hand on your lips, "this is what I use to kiss women and musical instruments, and to kiss you." Then, "This I used to breathe you in that first time, when you were afraid to speak, that day in the metro." "Have you known for that long?" "Before you did, even." You brushed my fingertips against your eyelids. "And these are what I see you with now, naked, the way God made you." "I'm scared, Arwa." "And here, where I had to cut my hair short to play the way I wanted and love the way I wanted. So I could heal." "Arwa, stop." "And then here, what you have to use to listen to my playing, and believe in it, every time as if it were the first." I was the first to fall in love, the first to announce my surrender in every conflict on earth, and Arwa, I was first in line to believe.

"Straighten up, Mariam, and let me see you, all of you." "I can't." "Okay, let's lie down on the floor, then, but let me see you. I can close the window if you're cold." "But I don't want to stop crying . . ." "That's okay. Let me see you, Mariam . . ." You wiped away my tears, and I said, without thinking, "You should've been Mariam, not me." "Never. You're Mariam, and you're perfect."

I was stripped bare in her hands. I couldn't stop crying until she started, and I gasped, "I'm not beautiful like you, Arwa," I stretched out on the ground atop my clothes, and the cold, like her, hugged us to its breast. She said, "You're the most beautiful woman on earth,

Mariam"; she repeated it with each piece of my body she tasted until I'd memorized its resonance and tones and the way my name flowed off her lips. I spent my night loving because, finally, I could.

3

It wasn't just about politics; it was something in the soul, entirely in the soul. I still know and believe and trust without anyone telling me to; I haven't really been a part of any of it, not the first demonstrations or those that followed, and maybe I never will. To the people who stayed in the square overnight, confronting the January cold with only a light jacket, however heavily it weighed on them—to them, I'm a traitor. And they have the right to feel that way. But you know it's not true. I took part in deeper things, like walking through long, dark streets that led nowhere, walking alone. Sometimes they were wet with rain and I slipped, then got up and fled from the stray shots fired by the police, the snipers' bullets, and harassment by thugs. I fled to fight better another day, my presence was light, like yours, and maybe that's what drew you. I shouted when I saw a government building, screamed with the anguish of my thousand years of isolation at every Egyptian flag I came across while people gathered to protect it; I withdrew from my already-depleted balance in life for the sake of a moment that was repeated everywhere I set foot. And I can't lie—the labyrinth of these streets? I loved it.

We moved from the Qasr El Nil Bridge toward the stone cake, that iconic plinth in Tahrir, turning at Bab el-Luq and finally reaching the gloomy atmosphere of Mohammed Mahmoud Street, facing the American University. I wasn't small and weak then; no, I had grown; I saw my humanity flying away from me like a balloon and happily bade it farewell. In rare moments, I came close to the saints, who are everywhere even though they're dead. I can exaggerate and say that, very occasionally, I felt I'd come close to the nature of God. Once, I raised my face to the sky without feeling the cold, without fearing the helicopter that demonstrators were saying would wipe us out. We were at once a multitude and utterly alone, and they betrayed us, throwing bombs at us, and masked police officers who looked like rats began to spread in every direction, and I suddenly feared they would break through our ranks. I was afraid and wept, returning to my own human skin. But even though the scene ended, I didn't lose hope; I felt the cold and loathed the labyrinth that made the daytime sky as dark as night, abandoning us or maybe sending us a message of abandonment. My fear grew and forced me back, so right away I retreated to my usual spot beneath a roof, sitting as still and quiet as a hundred-year-old woman, covering myself with a shawl to trick the cold. I knew that, on the inside, I would never warm up. I'm an obedient granddaughter with a family and a blind grandfather who follows with his ears the sounds emanating from the TV, relying on them as though they were his eyes. I'm luckier than him because at least I can see hands rising from the screen, see lips forming themselves into cries from gagged mouths; I can see and do nothing, just read the stream of presidential statements along with the TV reporters, long phrases on a blackboard rejecting what's happening, then acknowledging it, and nothing changes. They're all just like my grandmother, Arwa.

I've never believed my grandmother; not once in my life did I believe Umm Kalthoum. It's not because my mother warned me about her and then died due to her meddling—I would've hated her anyway. I know Baba never loved anyone like he loved his mother; I can hear him stating that fact baldly from the grave, where he can't tell a lie. Baba, you should've loved Mariam more, so that *I* could love Umm Kalthoum. I don't think he would've loved even my brother more than he did her. . . . He might have rocked him to sleep those first few months, rested his little head against his shoulder and sung sweetly to him the way I've seen fathers do with their kids on TV—but then what? I'm sure he'd have left him to Mama, forgetting him in her arms with a clear conscience and running off to fulfill his mother's wishes. Muhammad Ali loved Umm Kalthoum as though she were his daughter.

His undying love for her extended her life at the expense of Mama's, at the expense of his own. I understood as much the second I stepped onto Egyptian soil at the Cairo airport; when I walked out into the thick haze of this new country, I regretted not realizing it before. She was standing alone in a corner next to the glass doors, staring at the ceiling, her arms opened as though she were looking up at some god and praying. I recognized this stranger from the way her face matched Baba's; only a few days had passed since he'd said goodbye to me, since the goodbye to our home in Riyadh. I didn't have a single photo of him, only a few of my mother that Abdallah had found as he went through her things, which we'd divided between us. I hid them at the bottom of my carry-on's main compartment so that no one but me could find them because, as he said, that was the safest place in the world, and I forgot them there for years. I dragged the suitcase along with me, put it with the luggage of the family that looked out for me during the journey, picked it up from the line of bags alone, and took it through customs alone. I saw the others busy with their papers and with their own children and didn't say goodbye to anyone. I didn't feel guilty; I just went my own way after customs, walking next to other people like me, arriving to the homeland and scanning the crowd for people they didn't know. Then I bumped into her: the female version of Baba, a twin apparition standing there in front of me. She had his chin, his sleepy eyelids, his drooping brow, even his arrogant smile. When I laid eyes on her, his absence stung.

I became my own distinct entity; that's what I gained when I lost everything else. I became an individual, my identity not yet fixed but, without a doubt, specific to me. Because of the word "death," Arwa, the Mariam you love was born. The officer had to look at my picture and say my name before he let me pass, and I had to confirm it. "Yes, I'm Mariam." I signed forms to move from one point to the next in the vast airport, where I was greeted by black-clad women and men who'd been waiting for me for hours. They took my bag so I could walk unencumbered as I faced Cairo, defenseless, for the first time in my life. They asked, at a loss, about the coffin that hadn't arrived with the plane; I told them about Mr. Abdallah's decision to bury them together in the charity plot in Riyadh, and they reprimanded me for agreeing to it. All of this meant I had finally become me.

It was around then that I started using place names other people could recognize. Riyadh became Riyadh, not "home," and Cairo was Cairo, not "where my grandfather lives." I talked about people by defining who they were to me, especially my uncles, cousins, and aunts. I was forced to transform rapidly from the isolated girl I'd been into an attentive student of the world, recognizing, for example, that these people stationed at the airport, with their billowing galabeyas and that smell that frightened me, were my family, like it or not. It also meant understanding those words, "my family," as a final separation from Baba's and Mama's faces, and my own as I'd imagined it. That's why I lost sight of my image in the years that followed, wandering aimlessly in search of it in others' faces, trying to associate the absent with death, to separate myself from such a separation. For the first time, too, I understood the word "grandmother," a name I'd only ever heard on my parents' lips and which meant they'd forgotten I was there, and truly understood it as a living body, not just a voice on a cassette tape or some statue frozen in time and space. When I saw her, Sitti Umm Kalthoum, she stiffened, trying to decide what to do first, and I saw the questions in her eyes: Who was I? And what was I made of? She looked me up and down as though measuring me, down to the last inch. Otherwise, she didn't react, and I was drawn toward her without meaning to be, until she finally decided to embrace me.

In my first home in Cairo, I couldn't really take stock of my surroundings, even though Umm Kalthoum told me it would all be mine after the long life she would share with my grandfather. I sat when they asked me to sit and looked at them when they asked me to, and I had nothing to say about myself when guests came by the first day and demanded that I speak. I sat quietly like a pet dog next to my grandfather Ali, as he stroked my head and recited al-Fatiha, al-Muawwidhatayn, and Ayat al-Kursi. He was trying to protect me from evil, both visible and invisible, and he was depressed because he couldn't do it properly after losing his sight. As for my father's brothers, as the days passed and people came and went, I began to recognize them by how long they stayed when everyone else left. I was an orphan now, and everyone had to be kind to me; that's what the neighbors told my family. "Orphan" was my new name; in my first days here, I hardly ever heard the word "Mariam" on people's lips. Referring to me by my status was supposed to be noble, to compensate for having had my father and mother ripped away from me, a loss that still hadn't sunk in.

What you know now is what I was learning in stages as I made my way into my second life. I lost my parents so early, practically the moment I was born, and my childhood memories are colored by loneliness. The road the car took from the airport into the city scared me, and ended at the wasteland that laid ruin to my life: Masaken El Dobat. That was the sign marking the first neighborhood I would live in, the one I stayed in until I met you,

Arwa, and heard that you, too, had experienced tragedy there. As the car slipped into the darkness, I listened to my eldest uncle, Ammo Sulaiman, telling me that they'd used Baba's money to buy a quiet, isolated apartment out here where I could grow up and study to become a doctor, to save lives and make up for the ones my parents lost. Sulaiman tapped his walking stick on the vibrating footwell of the car, forcing me to look at him as he decided my future. I thought the road would never end; I kept remembering Abdallah's story about their death in an accident on a similar road, and I felt nauseous. The blessed relief of sleep evaded me, the sleep I'd always loved and that had loved me, and I gave myself over to my grandmother as she gently massaged my neck and held me close.

I couldn't smell anything now, but when the men got started talking in the Sa'idi dialect, the sounds of which I didn't like, I could make out the words but didn't understand and felt even more afraid. I wished the police in Riyadh had never asked to break down the metal door, I wished I'd been able to sleep for the whole drive and had never seen the road; I breathed with difficulty pressed against my grandmother's chest, felt her squeezing my hand over and over as though keeping time with the ticking of a clock. She kept whispering to me, in the midst of this desolation, "You don't have to be scared; it's okay," and I truly wanted to believe her, Arwa.

But believing Umm Kalthoum was beyond my very basic capacities, and still is. That first night, she decided to sleep next to me; the thing I'd always wished for with Mama came true here. She wrapped me up in a blanket that was heavier than I was, making me break out in a sweat before she'd even finished tucking me in. She hugged me again, asking me to relax, to sleep, not to worry. I remember the story she told me perfectly, despite my best efforts to forget. Egyptian Radio was announcing the broadcast of a new concert by Umm-Kalthoum-the-singer, and it was less than an hour before midnight when Umm-Kalthoum-my-grandmother decided to tell me her bedtime story about her namesake, the singer and national treasure.

I closed my eyes and saw the women huddled around me, each of them deciding to tell one another her story; the voices mingled, signaling to me again that I wasn't alone, and I lost myself in them. Then my heart thudded as the shimmering bubbles floated down around me. "I always wanted a daughter, Mariam. She would've been my secret-keeper, but your grandfather told me just one daughter would leave me 'divorced in no time flat'—all he had to do was say it three times, and it'd be final. I sat on the ground crying and telling the Lord that if I had even one girl, I would end up begging in the streets, and it wouldn't be fair—he wouldn't do that to me, would he? Years ago, they put me out in the streets to beg because I was a girl and because my father named me Umm Kalthoum. His little Thouma. Sallam, rest his soul, was the type who never stopped singing love songs. He wasn't like anyone else, and no one else was like him. My mother and I were the only girls in a house of ten men. An only daughter, and she told me that men were men and a girl was just a girl. And when I cried, Sallam would take me in his arms and tell me he could never love anyone the way he loved Umm Kalthoum.

He meant the singer's voice and how it echoed through the whole house and the houses around us. Some days I saw him crying as he listened to that voice of hers. Other times, I saw him laughing and laughing until his soul left his body and he fell to the ground feverish."

In those hours I spent between sleep and waking, the famed Umm Kalthoum didn't look like herself but like Shadia, the actress. She wasn't proud the way I would later see her in recordings of concerts, or the way she sounded in interviews; she came and sat next to me and started telling me the story of Sallam who loved her more than he did anyone else. *You don't choose love, Mariam; you don't choose to fall in love or be fallen in love with. People from the village knew, and could've sworn to you, that Sallam was crazy and had been for a long time, meaning that, for a long time, he'd been ready to fall in love. If you've got a bone to pick here, it's with God; take it up with him. . . . Ask your grandmother about Sallam's mother, who kept his shroud hidden for forty years after he was born, until he died and relieved her of the burden. Ask the villagers when Sallam ever went out to the fields with them. Then ask Umm Kalthoum how her mother could give birth to ten boys in just three years of marriage. Love is an act of God, Mariam.*

None of this was little Umm Kalthoum's fault, just as none of what happened to me was mine. We could've been friends in another time, could've played together, could've met Arwa together. At just four years old, Umm Kalthoum was already cleaning the whole house. Before she was born, her father could be heard praying for just one daughter so he could name her after his beloved, so that his name would forever be connected to hers. Umm Kalthoum Sallam. She would be his only joy. It wasn't just love for a singer, or love for song itself. Do you understand that, Arwa? Sallam loved Umm Kalthoum the way I love you, like my own soul.

And Sitti's whisper in my ear as I shivered there: "Love me, Mariam."

Because my condition kept getting worse, my grandfather started sleeping on my bedroom floor to fight off the winged djinn disguised as shimmering bubbles that were causing my illness. The incomprehensible, senseless illness. "Love me, Mariam." Words that were breathed into my body, raising my temperature, and Umm Mildam, Fever herself, couldn't be appeased, no matter how my grandfather pleaded or how hard I tried to comply. "Love me, Mariam. Because Sallam didn't love me, because he never loved anyone like he loved Umm Kalthoum, because he thought she could love him more than his daughter." He was wrong. Umm Kalthoum wouldn't love him more than she loved herself. After the boys grew up and disavowed their father to his face, the only story Sallam still cared about in all of Egypt was Umm Kalthoum's. She'd gone off to Cairo, he said, and eventually became the greatest singer in Egyptian history, like he always knew she would. Even before his boys grew up, he told this story with a tongue weighed down by sadness. By the time little Umm Kalthoum miraculously arrived in his life, he was an old man who could no longer see the hand in front of his face, and he finally felt that God loved him. He saw a meaning behind his torment. This little girl would understand him. God must have told her about him before he even created her. He was certain he would meet him soon, so he stopped caring who he spoke to, addressing himself only to the little girl, wanting to make her carry his few memories with his beloved so he could die in peace.

See, I've had to bear all that. I'll keep having to bear it. At the time, my back was nearly straight, but my grandmother reached out her hand to me, and I bent under the burden. For days, I lingered in semiconsciousness, and what happened before happened again; I completely lost touch with the real world and was taken to the hospital. I wore out the nurses, from one room to the next and one medicine to the next; my body turned into an old, punctured water bottle from all the holes punched in it, until my veins tried to flee my body, but in spite of all that, Umm Kalthoum wouldn't let me go. She called me the light of her life; we'd gotten closer since she told me her secret, she said. She would sit at the foot of my metal-framed bed at the Egyptian Railway Hospital and tell me in detail how everyone misused her, my father and her father, my mother and her mother.

Then the women started to visit, circling my body and enfolding me in their wings.

The women on neighboring beds, the naked Asian lady hand-in-hand with the inanimate, colorful princesses from Mario (though no Mario himself), and—of course—the oboist. The musician had pride of place among them, holding herself with the majesty of the Sphinx in pictures from before the French campaign, before its nose was broken by Napoleon. I close my eyes and remember her holding the oboe in her hands as though it were an infant or a rose. The oboist was the rose among the women in my life, its perfume her conspiratorial smile, in on everything I did with no questions asked. The others would join us over time, emerging from dreams, imaginings, and the reality of the sickbeds around me and their occupants' mothers, sisters, and wives, creating for me a whole world without men.

Back in the real world, my name splintered off and left me behind, leapfrogging from one class to the next. I got average grades, thanks to the large inheritance used to ensure my success, and I grew horizontally, stretched out atop my sheets. I didn't lose even a year from my "ordinary" life, but at the same time, I was trapped in a kind of solitary confinement, alone with my pain. As time passed, I discovered new types of pain, pain that coiled around itself like a snake and then struck, pain that spread through my bones and enveloped my fingers and toes; I felt it moving, licking my nerve endings, and I would start shaking. I told the nurses, but they didn't believe me. I said that the snake lived in my stomach, but the X-rays couldn't capture it. With time, I learned to recognize the warning signs, and eventually, the pain became less of a shock. The shimmering bubbles became part of my every experience. In this expanse of suffering, I saw my true kinship with Sallam.

He really did love her. Umm Kalthoum, that is, the object and final destination of all Sallam's love. If he asked her to bring him a drink of water, she would tell herself out loud that, this time, he wouldn't do it. But she delivered the cup with apprehension nonetheless, pulling back quickly before he could move, unaware that he was hiding the whip and that she'd be struck across the back as she turned to leave. He spoke submissively, reverently, "My darling Thouma!" She shouted it back at him: "My darling Thouma!" It was as though the beloved were a devil riding Sallam. His condition worsened over time, especially near the end, and the child Umm Kalthoum complied—what else could she do? Her mother didn't acknowledge her presence in the house, not in play nor in hunger; she said she'd had enough of her children ages ago. At just two years old, the little girl fed herself with her older brothers' leftovers and sometimes with insects, going out into the endless fields and eating everything she could reach. She ate even if she wasn't hungry because she would inevitably be hungry later that night, when there was no food to be had.

As she used to say, "Nobody's known misery like I have."

No one asked about her, even when she'd been gone for hours, even if she could've been devoured by wild animals; she always went back to the simple mattress at her brother's feet because she feared that death: gnashed between the teeth of wild beasts. "For my mother," she said, "it would've been a relief if I'd died." Then Sallam would show up, cursing the entire household, and take her to his room, to his fantasy of Umm Kalthoum, "Come, habibti; come, my love," and she would bow to his will and let him do as he wished.

In that jungle-like world, women undressed in front of me without permission, and watched me as I watched them. The walls were filled with images of them on their stomachs or backs, their legs spread wide and their chests arched, twisting and writhing and touching themselves as though they were in hell, and I found the fire seductive.

She was like a star, like the sun, luminous and warm, hope-inspiring, and the clouds swam around her. A shivering, earth-bound creature, he was drawn to the heat, to the shouts of those who revolved around her as she praised the Prophet like she could see him, tilting her head, smiling, flirtatious. She hadn't yet been visited by songs of love, nor had she sung "Amal hayati"; he drew close to her and burned, gladly. His heart sank back to earth, the sounds of the universe conspiring to spoil his pleasure, the birds in the trees, the cows grazing by watering holes all throughout the fragmented world, even the river in Munich, he tried to ignore them and just be present, with every fiber of his being he tried to stay there, just a few steps away from Umm Kalthoum.

He never thought of a way to reach her.

From the start, he knew she was a true star, that he would revolve around her all his life and never be anything to her but a simple passing human, like anyone else. Long years later, after he grew old extolling her name, the angel's lips brushing his ear every hour, *Umm Kalthoum, Umm Kalthoum*, and hearing the reproaches of his family—which turned with time into contempt, rejection, and finally a complete forgetting that there was ever something called Sallam—Sallam carried on, losing everything as she became more herself. Umm Kalthoum. Her name in lights and the daily headlines, the Star of the Orient, the radio announcer followed her every step on air, describing in detail every bead on the string around her neck, too shy to descend further. Long years later, Sallam would buy a ticket like everyone else to attend her concert in Cairo, in early March, the beginning of spring. He would enter the theater all fear and longing. *Years of separation and connection, Thouma, and nobody knows what I know.* He already knew she wouldn't recognize him; all he would get from her would be a long look, resigned and involuntary, otherworldly, one look at him among millions of looks in a single hour, and it would soon drift to focus on the ceiling, and she would finish singing to that ceiling as though it were the heavens, as though she saw God, and she would forget she ever saw him; he knew she would forget she saw him and that he would weep after all that time like he'd never wept before, he would be very sad and very happy, and that day his heart would cry out for death as a dear wish that would finally come true, he knew all this and consciously sought it out.

He departed as little Thouma played on the ground nearby; she didn't hear Azrael, the angel of death, ask, "All done?" Sallam insisted on putting the last bite of bread in his mouth, and all she heard was his response, "All done," then saw his head fall onto the low table as though someone had been carrying it and suddenly let go; the bite flew out of his mouth, and he died.

Her namesake would continue her meteoric rise, ignorant of the blood spilt, but Umm Kalthoum would grow up to rest in eternal misery.

Miserable because her son Muhammad, the only one among four boys who resembled a daughter in his softness and blind obedience, would grow up and need a woman, and that woman would be Siddiqa, her bitter rival, my mother. And because when her older brothers, students at Al-Azhar, saw Ali, they laughed and predicted that she would marry him and name their son Muhammad, thereby giving birth to another great Muhammad Ali Pasha, and when he knocked on their door on a hot summer afternoon ten years after Sallam's death, he took her away the moment he met her on the threshold, before she had washed herself of sweat or removed the excess hair from her body like other girls: Umm Kalthoum hadn't been dreaming of her wedding since birth. He dragged her after him, then outpaced her, walking ahead as she tried to catch up on long, strange, winding roads she'd never seen before, and she got lost and forgot her first life, Sallam and the big house, but she didn't forget that she was the second wife, following Ali's first and only love, whom he divorced when she couldn't give him children. "You know how your grandfather used to sleep with me in his prime? He would ask me to bend over. Put it in from behind. All while hollering the name of his first wife, Thuraya . . . It hurt, but I couldn't say no. And I couldn't avoid him. And when he fell down into bed next to me, wiped out, he would talk to her in his dreams, and I would hear the sound of both voices in one, saying, 'You're my life, my whole world,' like a slap in the face. If only I'd had a daughter, just one daughter, to tell my troubles to. I would've been better off. One girl. How did I give birth to five men? Well, we're Sa'idi. . . . I lost one son when he went abroad, and I'll be drinking from that bitter cup all my life—but God knows what he's doing! After all this time, he sends me the daughter who was taken from me. And she loves me, more than she loved Siddiqa. God sent me Mariam!"

She said my mother Siddiqa would take Baba's slippers off his feet as they watched TV and then bring them down suddenly on Umm Kalthoum's head; she couldn't defend herself, and no one intervened or stood up for her. That was early on in my mother's marriage to Muhammad, to scare my grandmother off and clear the room for Mama and Baba to sleep together comfortably; right after their wedding night, my mother had told Umm Kalthoum, "From now on, Muhammad is *my* husband and *my* son, he suckles from *my* breast, not yours." And she pulled her left breast out of her bra and flashed Umm Kalthoum.

All these scenes Sitti recreated for me, Arwa, how was I supposed to believe them?

It was beyond me. I couldn't believe it, and she didn't care; she continued to spin her stories day after day whether I believed them or not. She didn't even ask, and she didn't once look into my eyes as she was telling them, as if she were talking to a wall; all she cared about was talking, it's all she wanted: wash, iron, cook, curse, talk, talk, talk. She was still talking the day I left home to meet you, and the day I go back, she'll start all over, as if I'd never heard any of it, as if I didn't know, as if I were created for no other purpose than to listen. In every pause, start to finish, she would hang clothes on the laundry line as she harassed the neighbor ladies, cursing one and throwing good wishes the way of another. Based on her mood, she would pray, one day, for God to strike down the man selling rotten tomatoes and, the next day, that he would replace his wares with solid gold. She would scrub our balcony with soap and water, getting wet on the coldest days of the year, just to piss off the neighbor below us by splashing her sons' military uniforms with dirty water.

If anyone objected to her actions—if anyone dared to object—she would conjure up her old inner demon and scream and wail and tear her galabeya, holding up the mirror to the world's cruelty, branded on her flesh. She would pour out her wrath on the heavens, unashamed even of cursing God. They all feared her; if she dared to speak out against God, and so loudly, what could she do to mere humans? She would change her tone and summon the voices of grandmothers who died hundreds of years ago but still lived in her throat like unused vocal cords. Khadija daughter of Aamena daughter of Sabeeha daughter of Sitt Abuha. An endless family tree with no one but women, she summoned their strength to begin the next movement in her performance, resting for a time after the part in direct address, then arrived at Muhammad Ali, my father, and finally the djinn would depart, leaving her with her own voice. She lamented her son lavishly, his death in a foreign country crushed beneath the wheels of a car, and mentioned the abundant settlement that would never bring back his body or his scent. She remembered the dead of her entire family and mourned the likes of Sallam and her maternal and paternal uncles, not forgetting her mother, whom she cursed. Then she would turn to look inside and see my grandfather, who would not see her, so she pointed to his eyes, robbed of vision by his grief for Muhammad, and back to Muhammad she went, crying and whimpering, at which point she expected sympathy, but people closed their windows against her, turning a cold shoulder. Yet still she continued, reproaching God for his injustice, demanding a sacrifice from him in exchange for her love, crying and praying for revenge against the people on her street, in her building, and finally in her country; she wanted a sign from God to prove his divinity and might and quench her overwhelming thirst for destruction.

Once, she prayed for the world to end; a few years later, the revolution started.

Those were ordinary days, filled with disappointments like Christmas gifts, disappointments at work, in friendship, in love, climbing up the stairs, down the stairs, crossing crowded streets and empty ones, my imagination dim and not yet able to create; I pursed my lips and fixed my eyes on the ceiling and sleep came, I slept sixteen hours without a single dream, without changing position, greeting the world and bidding it farewell on my back; I examined bus drivers' faces, and my lips moved without the word "Tahrir" even coming out, I ignored my reflection in the plastic window of the microbus, my pulse dropping, speeding up, as we approached Abdul Monim Riad Square. I listened to the sound of wheels on asphalt, the yells of the street vendors, and I didn't relax until I knew there were no demonstrations, no alarm in people's faces, no smell of blood because still, anytime I had to walk near the museum, my ears strained to hear sounds from outside my field of vision, from around the bend in the sidewalk. After the scene with Central

Security and the word "down" repeated, I could no longer tell hallucination from reality, shots fired, people running toward me screaming, I could've been dropped by a rubber bullet, I could've been arrested just for entering the damn area, arrested, and left to die in detention, death seemed mandatory and inevitable; I saw officers rape female protestors, and horses trained to harass girls like me who entered the circle by accident; not once did I manage to separate fear from reality, I just kept walking, fighting to keep from staggering so I wouldn't seem drunk. Those were long, ordinary days, their only distinguishing moment *her* coming toward me, confident; in a white shirt and jeans, she crossed the street, her eyes fixed on my face and not the frenzied traffic, I don't know how she sensed my fear of crossing to the other side, I don't know how she knew me, her pale face and wispy hair indicating every possibility at once, her feet moving quickly as though she were trying to save a baby and the baby was on the other side of the street. I waited and watched the world pass by in the slow rhythm of a dream as she came up level with me, I buried my nose in the scent, sweat and perfume and something that spoke of the body, looked into her eyes as she approached and the image crystallized; she took my hand in hers and turned me around, two ballet dancers in a magical leap backstage, no one saw us crossing, the voice of the world died away, the moment seemed eternal; I wanted to lie down and sleep, smiling. She handed me off to safety and turned one final time, her eyes drifting across my speechless mouth; she kissed me on the cheek and left, and the voice of the world came back as she receded out of sight into the area around the museum. Those were ordinary days, filled with disappointments like Christmas gifts, disappointments at work, in friendship, in love, climbing up the stairs, down the stairs, crossing crowded streets and empty ones; those were my days before I met you, Arwa.

Everything repeats to send you a message you don't want to receive; everything has repeated since you were a small heart beating in your mother's womb. It was only natural for the blow to come from where you least expected it, natural for it to come from the road, Champollion Street itself, the most familiar place in the world to you because it abandoned you, the spot you passed on your way to Mahmoud Bassiouny Street before deciding to cross, ignoring the tanks and rifles, ignoring the officers carrying Molotov cocktails emerging from streets whose names you didn't know. You were there and you weren't, a leaf on the surface of the river, leaving the world behind and floating to the microbus stop, and why? Just so I could go back home, so I could go back home. "Home," which meant seclusion and trying to write poems, steeping them in all my ennui and illness. Fail and start over, fail and start over. I've spent my whole life trying, I truly wanted to be a poet, to write a whole collection about the ghagariya woman, to attempt a poem about the oboe player, engraving into it what I knew so long ago and forgot, before I forgot completely and there was actually nothing left for me to tell of her story, what her story was with me. I still don't understand anything; even today, after all this time, I can only be described as naïve. But then you showed up, as though the movie whose months of previews had left me dazed in anticipation, the magic movie that would end suffering in a flurry of wings, would be shown in your home. I wanted to come here and to see, Arwa, there was something of the cinema about you, and something of my poems, something I hadn't written yet . . . but that doesn't mean I understood it; in no way, Arwa, does it mean that.

Like everyone else in the country, I thought this was it, the world had changed and all that was left was to go home, because there was nothing else to do; seven thousand years after the pyramids were built, how were you supposed to know that no one had ever actually wanted the solution, that it was still an unknown? Who would sneak us the correct answer if the angel skipped the exam? We suddenly realized that angels don't meddle in human affairs, and the knowledge pained us; you were left to experience it alone, you would learn your lesson only by failing, the disappointment was unbearable for the whole country, but you had to bear it, had to chafe against the burden for some unspecified time, maybe your whole life. However I rationalize it to you or to them, the only truth was me standing naked before you in that apartment, with all the helplessness of a single mouth for all the rivers of the world, flooded against my will, powerless to resist. Arwa, I have excuses you wouldn't believe if I tried to say them out loud. That day, all I needed were your eyes to feel I was a woman, and whole. I could've leapt for my clothes and left elated by such an easy victory, but you, no, you would've considered your time with me wasted, told yourself you should've been out in the square under that dark sky with your oboe and your thick black jacket from Germany, calming yourself enough to play and amuse them, telling of the pain that would pass and the death that would pass, and the revolution would be immortalized in your music and the hope you brought from the colorful Alps. I was just a black-and-white photograph; I would never be your girl, before this I'd had nothing to do with that part of life. For the longest time, I froze up around my grandfather and surrendered to my grandmother's theatrics with silence and apologies for my sins and everyone else's; I would've done the same with the police if they'd locked me up, on purpose or by mistake. I felt like a parasite, begging for my food, money, and a roof over my head in winter; my life was meaningless, and not only was I dull, but I had no voice with which to demand love. I was absolutely nothing.

The two contrasting images made the little girl in me cry. She'd boarded the massive plane that day thinking she'd never make it back to solid ground; the clouds were like a sea outside her window, with no beginning and no end. First was the painted image of the girl with wings who died a thousand times in the square without really dying and, second, a miniature image of my helpless mother praying God would bless her with a boy to please her husband: just one boy, that's all, the one she would never be blessed with. The little girl kept crying; she'd come back to Egypt and lived a second life that was no different from the first, but she'd chosen to ignore that. Life ignored me and taught me to ignore myself. But now at least I can go. I know my place in the world, and I'm fine knowing you'll pull the worn-out deadbolt behind me and sleep in comfortable darkness here or behind the half-open bedroom door, no one invading your privacy, no fear because the light comes from within and you're tired and have a hard day ahead fanning the flames of revolution. Why didn't I get it when you first took me back to the bus stop? Why didn't I realize that you saw me the way I saw myself when the doctor tossed me aside at birth, just one of a hundred other children? You knew the end of the story and decided your time was too precious to make a go of it with someone like me. A disappointment that would only bring more disappointments. I don't think you know what that tastes like, and I don't want you to. Why did I break? I don't know. I was so sure about it all, and I gave in, told the simplest truth there was, unafraid, "I want to go," like a little girl to her mother as she lies dying.

I said it, "I want to go," as we lay on the floor atop an old navy-blue rug, I said it and suddenly noticed how saturated the color was and felt sad, my gaze drifting to the darkness outside the open window overlooking a road like the one I used to run down in my dreams before waking up beside my blind grandfather. Your eyes grew brighter, and you closed them wearily, and the color of your lips, recently so vibrant because of me, faded. Imagine everything I lost because of a single phrase, imagine how I blew myself up for no one. Then you turned away, you took it kneeling, like Mowgli, who was raised by animals in the jungle, with the same dignity, grief, and decisiveness. You didn't ask me any questions, Arwa, or argue with me, and it was torture, in that moment and in my memory of it later. You backed away, went into attack or defense mode, I'm not sure which, and to me, it felt both sudden and slow motion.

You sat back on cramped knees, tilting your face to the sky. I brought you all this unhappiness, love—*I* did. You weren't sobbing and whimpering the way I do when I'm upset, just weeping silently; I looked at you and told myself there was no reason for you to cry, and again I saw the image of myself as a child on the plane and wanted to scream: *I'm not that important*! For the first time, believing that was exhausting. Can neither of us remember how much time passed, how much of the night was wasted? "Don't go now; wait till morning, it's warm in the bedroom." Then you added something that stung: "And get dressed." I remembered that I was naked and tried to cover my body with my hands, which suddenly felt foreign; your words forbade me my clothes, forbade me to sit, stand, walk, run; Arwa, I wished I could simply freeze.

It's Arwa. Thin, pale, light-footed, she walks in splendor like a quill in an inkwell, sometimes in a short skirt that the wind whips about at will, unintentionally accentuating the image, a boy in the body of a woman, the most beautiful young man in creation hidden in Arwa's body. When she moves she leaves a void between her legs, legs that torment anyone who can't lie between them, I burn in that void when she runs from me, naked, in the apartment on Champollion Street and teaches me to run after her, to love, her back taut, all her muscles tensed for a single touch before she cries out. It's Arwa who taught me how God arranged the universe.

Looking at her seated, leaning against the wall as I was supposed to leave, I saw the fine blonde hairs scattered across the two lines of her thighs, and I saw the pores beneath them from where I was; without her seeing me, I lifted my hand in the air as she wept, and I began to feel out what I imagined to be the keys on an oboe. That's when I decided to stay, not to leave ever, to wrap myself in all the sadness that shaped her in Europe and hold it within me. I knew the blessing of her presence even when I refused; she didn't force me. I was at her house at night, during the revolution, I played with her and then had enough of our games, and she, who'd lived in Germany, sank to the ground, edging toward the oboe lying innocuously between us, so blissfully unaware that I'd hurt its owner; I'll live off that image of her, violently pale, spilling, spilling over with tears as she picked up the oboe as though saying not just to me but to the whole world, *Enough!*

I wasn't the object of that sadness, Arwa, but I wanted it to end with me. I know now that I was drawn to you as like to like. I couldn't stop tears that I didn't start, but I wept with you simply because weeping was—and always will be—all we could do. My eyes retained a thousand images of you in that one glance: the present, tomorrow, the future when we would part ways. I saw how I would die of the torment and would've trod on burning coals to apologize. It's Arwa. Her voice is as soft as her footsteps and her skin and curls, singular and unforgettable as a warm iron passed over silk, leaving behind it the shadow of a letter impressed on its purity. Her voice is like a veil when she speaks, in summer or winter, dancing in complaint and in love, especially in love, when it twists and tumbles to delight and entertain. Arwa wept in a way I didn't know existed, and it made me think back on all the people I'd seen cry throughout my life, on TV, in the movies, in poetry, no one wept tears like rain the way you did, even the muscles in your chest were trembling and alert. So I took heart, watching the moment unfold. Arwa forgot me, she didn't listen to me crying, she pulled away from me, and I felt I saw her fly out the window and disappear into the darkness, naked and oblivious to the cold. The possibility of that loss was the greatest in my life, and it shattered me; I couldn't bear it, even in theory. I'm not saying that my mind acted right away to come up with a new plan; what I'm saying is that her sadness constituted a deed, whether good or bad, and mine was another, and our salty lips were the best intercessors for us in hell.

Before Arwa began playing, I stood up, swaying; my joints cracked, and I wished I would fall to pieces there in front of her so she would forgive me. I leaned against the walls and then made her watch me as I walked away; my back wasn't as symmetrical as hers, but it did its best to keep me upright. I staggered, aboard a ship on choppy seas, and made it to the living room just to pitch over. Pushing open the bedroom door, I sought shelter in the darkness. The warmth of the bed reached up to my hunched form, and immediately I sensed that there were others present I didn't know, ghosts, I thought, since I couldn't see them, the scent of their sweat thick in the room, or perhaps people who'd been breathing heavily and then hidden themselves, and now there was no one left. These are the reasons you live in the dark, Arwa, aren't they? I didn't speak, didn't look for the light switch, I existed on the little bit of light that reached me from the oboe room until I touched the large, low mattress. I pulled a heavy comforter over my legs, one big enough for two people and which smelled like them, and I'd wrapped myself up between them when, all at once, the oboe in the next room cried out in song, one I would later learn was by a Greek composer, a woman. Arwa loved her. The music was harsh and filled with a rebuke for anyone who has ever left. I gasped, afraid, and pressed my hands to my ears, wishing I could lose my hearing. I nearly wet myself like a child, and I could see her in my mind's eye issuing the order, firm: "Get dressed."

"Arwa, come here." I begged her with all the life in me, repeating the phrase over and over with a vengeance, no different from the bullets fired repeatedly nearby. My fear increased, so I raised my voice above the sound of the oboe. Arwa persevered, and so did I. "Please, come here."

"Arwa, come *here*!"

I'd begun to feel feverish. Looking around, I saw a tanned man with long hair and a pale woman embracing, found myself caught in their embrace. I realized they were her loved ones, and I hurriedly asked them to intercede for me; in response, they whispered to me the words I could die happy hearing:

"Arwa, Arwa, Arwa."

Finally, the oboe went silent. I felt it slide to the ground and fall asleep, and I was jealous. The familiar scent of sweat wafted toward me, cutting through the fear, and I was jealous. The two beings in the room had a scent, and she was their daughter; this I knew. My body clung to the smell, sniffing and licking it like a dog.

It's Arwa. After the first embrace of forgiveness, I asked her to turn on the light; she obeyed me without thinking, sinking away from my body, and I regretted asking and walked with her to the light switch on the wall. I wasn't stalling, I just wanted to see, and again she said, "Take it off." To avoid making the same mistake twice, I didn't ask what I was missing, I didn't tell her we were both already naked, I saw how serious she was and surrendered. I didn't look around to be sure we were alone as her eyes shifted from my body to empty space, and when the darkness was illuminated, the bed was simple again, a traveler's bed, questions sprang to mind and answers flowed as we stepped into the cool covers, and I whispered to them that we would warm them. Arwa wrapped me up the way they swaddle newborns, the only difference being that she kissed me all over as she did so, drank me in with her gaze as though caressing me with her eyes. Her absolving touch as she adjusted my limbs on the bed and covered me made me want to give more of my skin to her, never hiding myself, and she was satisfied and slipped under the blanket next to me. I parted my legs easily, and she slid hers between them; I quieted as she positioned herself like the summit of a pyramid or a crown atop me, but we didn't melt into one another until finally the morning came and the sounds of gunfire in the street faded; we held each other like the man and woman I'd seen before, but in our own way, remaining awake, aware, as they slept.

"You won't get away this time."

I looked at you, Arwa, and I saw life in yellows, reds, and greens, as if we were living in a tent in the desert, just us. I saw your face as a shining light, and I hid my eyes in your neck because of its brilliance, the heady scent of your body overtaking me, crushing me like a tank in the street, so I said something, anything: "Did you close that window?" But you cried out, your eyes shining, "Do you love me?" I stretched out my left hand, so close to you, because your eyes were regaining their joy and forgetting their tears.

I came closer and nuzzled her nose playfully, I touched her nose and lips with my index finger, then traced her face, as people do with something sacred. I wanted to believe that Arwa was real, warm-blooded, and alive. *Arwa is real, warm-blooded, and alive, Mariam.* The whites of her eyes were tinted pink with desire for me, the green of her irises shifting gray, hazel, and blue, then dark again, as though they had a will of their own, outside the laws of nature; with every kiss that sewed our lips together, the taste of my saliva changed, becoming something forever different since our first kiss. Arwa made me gasp in response like someone drowning in the sea, clawing for a life preserver: "Yes, I love you." I waited for her rebuke as though it was words of love, for her breath on my neck: "And if you try to run again?"

"Arwa, kill me if I try to run again." Even the thought of you killing me excited me. I'd become a different person from the one who'd walked into your apartment, who climbed the stairs and told you no. A sharp divergence from my life to the life I hadn't known I wanted.

It's Arwa I touched, her bones and skin beneath my fingertips, I felt her reed-like arms, the network of veins and arteries connecting the chest to the abdomen to everything in her I couldn't name that made me dizzy. Why should I name it? The sense of touch drove me wild as I discovered anticipation like the first two humans discovering it for the first time. My hand turned blue as I moved it away from her face and back again, I was a dead girl, dead or dying; her frame covered me as I closed my legs beneath her and opened them again instinctively, and she moved against me. She placed her head between my breasts.

You'd taken off your shirt in that room, and I'd forgotten how to breathe when I saw your breasts, not because I didn't expect them but because they were more perfect than I knew. I opened up to my craving for you so quickly I surprised myself; I'd never known desire for a woman, I'd never known desire at all. The slight curves of your breasts were barely visible from afar, like I said, a boy in a woman's body, nipples the color of your tongue, the color of your inner flesh, hard and alert, threatening delicious injury. In this moment, now, I paused, stunned, wanted to experience them with my nails, teeth, nose, tongue, in every way possible. I was lost in thought long enough to feel embarrassed, and I wanted to hide but didn't have time. You'd stretched out atop me as though making my body your bed; I felt your nipples stab my ribcage, felt the stabbing reach my lungs, and my breath became ragged.

It's Arwa. She reminded me what it meant to be naked all this time, in music and in rebuke, in bullets as they grew louder and more insistent nearby; at another time, I would've killed myself, just the idea of Arwa made me tremble. At first, I was rocked by sadness when you opened the door for me and ushered me into your darkness, moving me in unfamiliar directions. But you took hold of me. Now every part of me was cherished.

Her head, conspiratorial, didn't stop to nestle against me, but her tongue began to caress a spot in the middle of my chest she knew well, where the spirit is. I was dragged back and collapsed as she continued excavating, looking for my roots. She bit down gently, and I wished she would be violent, she was trying to draw me out, to mine me as one does a precious stone. Arwa, the slightest resistance would've left a noticeable mark upon my flesh; Arwa grasped the spot with her teeth, and I could hear the blood boiling in my ears, crashing like the sea from shore to shore inside my head. I fragmented further, resisted rather than surrender. Floundering and searching for her eyes, for calm, I cried out to her, "Look at me!" No one told me what to do, and I wasn't afraid of disappointment; for the first time, I turned and ran at full tilt into the jungle.

"Look at me, Arwa."

My heart thudded as Arwa's head rose in response; these were not her eyes, they were as large as the sun in my childhood drawings, so large and frightening that I wanted to hide in them from myself and from Arwa, but she didn't give me time. The sun shrank and took aim at my chest. My heart began to beat wildly, I couldn't move or see, I closed my eyes and let myself go, kept going in a time outside of time, with no limits or beginning; how short my life was, how short it would be, with no meaning except for this moment.

"Your breast."

My body became a heart, a heart the size of a monstrous human being, beating to the sound of the word falling from her tongue, I writhed as hell cracked open deep within me, I swear it was burning, burning, burning still brighter. Another fire in her eyes when I opened mine, a wood fire and angels working in the flames; I swear I saw them in those few moments of clarity.

"Mariam, your breast."

The pleasure she took in the word. Subtle. Arwa taught me to play down pleasure, to never get enough, between wanting her to put out the fire and wanting her to continue, I was grasping something new about giving: extravagance. "Let me suckle from your breast, Mariam, like you're my mother." Her mouth was already where it needed to be. She had full permission, but what I granted her at that moment contained an entire alternate history of my life, one that could only be called revolution. "Do it," I said, and "I love you." I cupped her face in my palms and pulled her closer. With those words, Arwa, you were taking back your Egyptian identity, weren't you? Yes. A forgotten Egyptian woman, face exposed, with neither veil nor modesty. Right? Of course. You ate from my womb and felt pain. "I love you." How many times had this room heard those words, *I love you*? How many people had lived and died without hearing them spoken in such a straightforward and soothing way, so free of deception.

This building has stood here since it was first built, on the corner of this alley off Champollion, rejecting the cruelty of downtown and its one-eyed history. Close by, people die of hunger to avoid a bullet, and others die from a bullet to escape the cold; it's where I died and you died, among countless other humans who, for better or worse, we weren't: we all arrived here together. Eat, my love. I feel your nourishment coming from my belly, Arwa, and I feel my spirit rising. I will mourn all the loveless dead in all the world.

"Enter into me, Arwa."

Because this thing between us is forever, life must cradle it like an only child, one it will never stop pampering. We heard someone scream outside, someone alone; he stopped after what seemed like a long run coming from some distant street, maybe Mohammed Mahmoud Street itself or Tahrir Square, or maybe from the High Court where we met up that first time; his choked breathing made it clear how he'd suffered on the way. He hid in the entrance to our building on Champollion, afraid of people who'd been following him for ages, and when they appeared, they were legion, and like him, we were afraid. They arrived silent and confused, looking about them in vain, no sound ringing out but the thump of their military boots on the courtyard tiles. They frightened the birds in Munich. We saw the intransigeance, the tyranny, the certainty that they were above us all; we didn't see where they got it from, we were just afraid. They flushed him out, surrounded him, and kicked him to the ground; they did it carelessly, as though all they'd done was intercept an Al Ahly player to get the football back. We saw him bounce disoriented between the walls of the prison they had built with their bodies; he banged his head against their bones, but of course no path opened for him. He must have seen the gloating smirks devolve into panting; they were demented guard dogs. He knew the fate they wanted for him was coming, so he fought his last battle, the battle for his honor; he couldn't survive it, though he'd done everything he could for thousands of years.

"Enter into me, Arwa. Don't leave me. Don't send me out there."

If we'd opened the wooden window that had been closed for ten years, we could've watched them smacking him around, one after the other. He was too proud to scream; the only signs of his pain were the violent jerking of his body and the gasps he let out each time he imagined they would let up; we would've seen one of them take out his service weapon and stick it somewhere intimate, hidden, on his body, then fire six times in succession, even after the first shot felled him, from despair, not death. Arwa wasn't frightened like me; she'd already seen how hideous life could be, and nothing surprised her now, so I sought refuge in her. The hand that held the weapon followed the body as it fell, continuing to take aim at the corpse, now yielding, dead. He was really dead. As I lay beneath her, helpless, I inquired, "Did he die?" as they dragged him to the pile of garbage bags at the far corner of the apartment building, legs all moving together like a pack of mangy dogs that had worn themselves out in pursuit of a mouse. The men who killed him dragged him away from our window without our even asking. *Where is everyone, Arwa?*

What happened didn't frighten anyone but me, and the easiest thing was to pretend I wasn't frightened, so I did, and then Arwa didn't give me the chance to be scared; her madness flared up, and she began kissing me passionately and licking me, her body quivering, glistening with beads of sweat. She startled me by standing upright on the bed, her spine like an arrow whose pale form and warm features restored my self-love. I was alarmed for her and called out again: "Arwa?" I saw her as pure and unadulterated as though she'd been born an hour ago, with that first redness and bulging of veins; she was so tall I thought her head would pierce the ceiling. Then slowly she came back down to me, to her knees, her breath grew ragged as she spread her fingers between my legs and positioned herself against me, opening her legs and pressing her inner sanctum against mine. At the first touch, a sharp intake of breath, dizzy; she turned her eyes away from me, and I closed mine as she began to grind against me. I told her, "I can't take it, Arwa," and she responded by rocking her body faster, harder. "Tell me you love me, Arwa." "I love you, Mariam," and then she was pounding against me the way they pound wheat in the countryside, with the same intensity and hope, torment and pain; we did not open our eyes, and we did not see.

Mariam, It's Arwa

You were on the metro platform. Your hair was in a crooked ponytail, and you were staring into space and smiling to yourself. You didn't know you were smiling, and nobody sitting nearby pointed it out. That's when I knew you didn't have a mother, or a boyfriend, or any friends. That you were a simple girl who didn't know how beautiful she was yet. Beautiful, and totally unique. Would you believe me if I told you that? I could've sworn you had a musical instrument with you, hidden away in a bag, or maybe a paintbrush. When your eyes met mine, you let them linger for a moment, toying with me. I got up, and a nervous smile spread over my face without asking permission. Something in you shone, oblivious to the effect it had. It was twice as bright because you were clueless about it, and that combination of cluelessness and impishness made me burn for you. I stepped out of the metro car, forgetting the incident with the soldiers like it never happened, returning suddenly to the pleasure of finding myself in Egypt. A very old Egypt I'd only seen for a moment in my life before it was forgotten, making me wonder if I'd imagined it. I wasted my youth looking for it. Your Egypt was different, and I craved it without realizing it. That's when I remembered that Egypt wasn't Munich. Busking didn't work here. Meanwhile, if it was up to you, you'd have kept playing your game till morning. Just playing and running around. My nerve endings burned, and I walked toward you. I'd never been with an Egyptian woman. I was terrified of myself and, despite that terror, couldn't take my eyes off you. I fell in love first. Did I know what love meant? Did I know *how* to love? Did I know better than you what love meant in Egypt? But you were like a white rose that would bloom in spring. . . . You had the promise of life about you, and I was scared for you, of what I might do to you. And every time that fear popped into my head, I saw you leap in front of me, protesting, shouting that we could rewind life and start over, you knew how. You asked me about the oboe, and I answered. I should've opened up to you and let you convince me to stop spending my nights on the streets. When I told you, "You remind me of the people I love," I bent the truth. Really, I saw you here, in the apartment. Naked and wrapped around my body. Fire swept through me, and my breathing quickened—like playing the oboe, the more I exhaled, the louder the sound. I lost my footing, Mariam, I lost my footing, and the current carried me away.

Mariam, the apartment on Champollion Street is the one I was supposed to be born in, back when my second name was announced correctly in the newspapers: Arwa Michel, after my real father. Not Arwa Salah. After that, God created people, and they changed the stars. He created religions and injustice and Egypt and its politics, built Salah El-Adl, and made my mom's parents Muslim.

The only way to cancel out the unnatural equation was for Sara to commit suicide when she was pregnant with me. As for solving the problem of Michel, that was the result of a warped mind. Imagine if we all died the way he did. We'd go up on the roof, yell down to the cowardly doorman and laugh at him, then take off like rockets. Our bodies might give him nightmares, all piled on the ground and swimming in blood. He might feel guilt.

It went down like it always does, Mariam. Sara was a rose among the girls at university and didn't care what others thought of her. In summer, she went everywhere in a skirt and a yellow, green, or red blouse, her arms and legs bare. She walked in a way that wasn't meant to be flirty. Wasn't meant for other people. Sometimes she'd bury her nose in a book of poetry and walk like she was walking on its verses and not the dirty streets. She didn't notice when people's jaws dropped as she passed. They were ready to believe anything except that in Cairo, a woman could simply walk. They said, "No way she's Egyptian," the way they say that about me. And they were right. The story goes that when Napoleon got to Egypt with his army, one of his men deserted. He fell in love with one of my grandmothers, learned Arabic, and disguised himself. He took a Muslim name. A real looker who died early and left no trace except for his green eyes and his French physique, like a stamp on his offspring. Sara got a generous share of that inheritance and Arwa a little bit after her. All because of love. When Michel made love to Sara. But Sara was more beautiful than Arwa, Mariam; the Virgin in this picture can attest to that.

Sara didn't leave Egypt. She didn't run away like me, even when she could see her destiny getting impatient, calling to her more eagerly every day. She read Proust and Colette and spent her evenings talking to classmates about a Godard film that had dazzled her. She looked down her nose at them as she spoke about the film. *Vivre sa vie.* They shrieked when they saw a picture of the main character, a young woman with short hair like Sara. And they thought to themselves that Sara was prettier than the actress. They snuck glances at her body in the film stills and touched them as if they could touch Sara. Then they touched themselves and fantasized about that woman, amazing and naked and killed by a cowardly stray bullet. Like Sara.

In the summer, she tied her hair back in a pink or pale blue bow to protect it from the dust kicked up by factories, cigarette smoke, and smog. She wore whatever colors she wanted, and people resented how effortless her beauty was. At university, Sara was a queen among the other girls. She stood in the blistering sun without an umbrella. Here she is, surrounded by the other girls in her class, laughing for the camera. Though, honestly? She didn't even see the camera, or the other girls. When she wasn't around, they called her stuck-up. She would hide her shyness by lifting her chin, and her head would tilt ever so slightly, like she was about to smile but then didn't. You'd beg her to do it, just do it, to release what was trapped in your blood. Or her blood. I know that because I used to do the same thing. I still do, any time I feel like I'm trapped in my own mind but too proud to scream. Like you did that day in the metro, the way you tortured me. The way I played in the metro, surrounded by all those people, torturing the soldiers.

Look at these pictures! The truth is, Sara was sick of lectures. She would've been happy to just stay home alone and read. That way no one would ask questions she didn't want the answers to, about literary periods or the etymology of some word, or about some grammar rule. Everything Sara knew, she knew by feeling; the tongue couldn't translate it.

One day, she fell asleep in her dark lecture hall after the professor and the other students had left. No one stumbled across the forgotten girl, and it's not like she had a cell phone people could reach her with, not like you did yesterday. Even the janitor overlooked the body stretched out in the rows of seats. *I dreamed I was in a deep sea but couldn't drown.* Sara opened her eyes terrified and saw darkness and confinement and two black eyes staring back at her. *I said, "Are you the angel of death?"* He was startled. "No, I'm Michel." *It was the first time I'd seen him, this poor guy,* definitely *not an angel.* Sara gave Michel a look he read as contempt, so he decided to give her a lecture, more affecting than any she'd gotten at uni: "A fine lady like yourself could've up and died here if not for Michel the carpenter, and you're looking down on him?" He worked some magic on the locked wooden door to the courtyard and opened it, then turned his back to her. He left her there as the afternoon sun fell all at once onto her sheer dress. Hell burned Sara's refined eyes as though they'd never seen the sun.

She called after him. "Hey, carpenter!" Asked him to come back. Just till she could face the blazing disk on her own. Just till she believed that, dream or no dream, she could drown like the rest of creation. He was gaunt and tan, and his long hair was tied at the nape of his neck. *He had a hump other people rarely noticed and a slight limp—he had a wooden leg, Arwa!* He was walking away from her, limping and limping, not leaning on anything or anyone. *He was our age, Arwa, but also way older; he was the oldest person on earth.* One of those poor guys who built the mighty pyramids, ordered to be ignored as they dropped, exhausted, from the scaffolding. The pharaoh insisted the work continue, and they were left there to die. *He was a miracle walking on earth, and I followed him.* By the time she reached the light, he'd disappeared, leaving Sara with nothing but his name and his trade.

Michel the carpenter. She knew he was a student there, too, but his strange brand of magic made it clear to her what "Michel the carpenter" meant. Michel wasn't like anyone she knew, either in her family or in French movies. He was a being who could make you open Baudelaire's great book of poetry and read about the moon and hatred and rancor, and then dream. And Mariam, Sara realized she'd never dreamed before Michel. She lay on her stomach and read and suddenly felt like it was Michel who wrote the words, all the words in all the books in the world. *You fooled me . . . What a shock that was. It was like you were two different people, and you kept eluding me.* Other times, he existed as three people. Once, he disguised himself as a little boy heading to school in the morning, carrying a burlap bag with no books. She saw him everywhere and got flustered, a headache leaping to the top of her skull. She felt like the world would never go back to what it was before she met the carpenter and that she needed to drown.

Suddenly, you remembered your inheritance when it came to love: marble stairs and the obsessive words of your parents ringing in your chest: "Sara will be a French teacher at the fanciest schools, and officers will court her favor." The space between what you'd learned and what you'd experienced suddenly felt immense. A black hole you hoped would swallow you up. In old photos, Michel looks like a guardian of looted antiquities. Like the Sphinx on old postage stamps. After its nose was broken, of course. One look at that bum, and life turned upside down. *If Mama had seen him, she'd have called him a bum, and my heart would've ached.* Mariam, heartache's the direct result of believing poetry. No matter where you're from, that's how it happens; nothing comes for free.

She asked around about him at uni. Days spinning around days as though the earth had split open and swallowed him up, not leaving so much as an eyelash. It seemed almost plausible that he was some supernatural being she wouldn't see again. Or that this was a scene from a play and he was an actor. Could it all have been a dream? His name was Michel the carpenter. So she asked around about him. Michel the carpenter was a Christian student in the Philosophy Department and a name in the State Security register. "He's under surveillance, Sara, keep your distance." "He's just a kid, but he thinks he's this great revolutionary who'll change the world." "He's a nobody; what does a girl like you want with him?" At a demonstration, he stood in front of a security officer and shouted the immortal words of Ahmed Urabi, "We are slaves to no one and will be inherited no longer!" So they dragged him around by his shirt in front of everyone and left him there vomiting while people laughed. *It was the talk of campus, but even hearing about him drew me to him.* Everywhere she went, Sara stood in front of the mirror. *My clothes are boring, what if they gross him out. My body's too skinny, too French; Egyptians don't like it!*

And you were totally illiterate when it came to Egyptian culture. What did you know about Ahmed Shawqi's poetry, for example? *Who was Ahmed Shawqi?* What did you know about Umm Kalthoum? *I never liked Umm Kalthoum.* Everything, everything was French! *What would I tell him if I saw him again?* You would at least thank him, Sara. If not for him, you'd have turned into a wax statue from sleeping too much, shut up inside that building. *I thanked him! I went to the Philosophy Department and asked if I could take him to the movies. I was so nervous I was shaking, Arwa.*

Michel looked at her as though he'd never met her before, as though he were paranoid or had Alzheimer's. "I don't like movies." And he straightened his back and crossed his arms over his chest. Sara smiled uneasily. Whenever nothing, not a single word, popped into her head, that's what she did, she got embarrassed and smiled. She found the word she wanted as he turned to go. "Sorry." "Me, too," he said. Then he hurried off, not intending to come back, no matter what.

He was a man of his word. No matter what, he wouldn't come back. He kept his distance on one leg made of flesh and bone and one lame leg. But Sara was the sort of woman who broke her promises. She turned onto the street of mechanics and workshops, filled with muscular men and shouting and general hubbub. It's where Michel lived. She made her way down the street, following the description she'd gotten from university security and the address in the student disciplinary records.

Their workshop was on a street that was really a glorified alley. A father-and-sons carpentry workshop. It was the size of the smallest bathroom in the palace you lived in. And in the middle of it was a modest painting of the Virgin holding her son, flanked by her husband Yousef, also a carpenter, his face lit up by gratitude. You could pinpoint the workshop from the sound of the saw. From a distance. The sound of the knee joint struggling against the ground. You were attracted to it like the murmur of the Isar River. Like the Isar when Arwa spent all those years on its banks and then came back. The sound spoke of a love of carving. He could spend his whole life working with wood. And Mariam, that carving was so much like music!

Sara walked unsteadily, trembling. The main street was like summer, but the inner alley was absolute hell. By the time she reached the workshop, she felt like she was melting. She'd left home without deciding what she was going to say to him. She would let the scene play itself out. I mean, what could possibly happen that hadn't already?

Your style was *the* style. The white skirt and blue sleeveless blouse, a black silk scarf falling away from your shoulders as you entered, suddenly appearing in the doorway like a movie star. You'd just found out that Champollion Street had nothing to do with the French. Except for Youssef Chahine's office at the end of the street; *that* had something to do with the movies. You liked the smell of koshary and decided then and there to treat him to some when you found him. And to apologize, Sara. It occurred to you how important it was to apologize. You could figure out what you were apologizing for later, n'est-ce pas?

Abou Tarek's koshary shop was the crossroads of the world those days. Or at least it seemed that way to Sara. She'd heard about it in the movies. In conversations. But she hadn't been allowed to go. A diktat of class. And because she was a lady, and attractive. The sound of metal cups clinking as she wended through the tables, bumping into them. The bottles of dukka that everyone held, people who washed their hands and people who didn't. And the spoons in the symphony of war, an everyday war waged by the human race that she was totally oblivious to. If her eyelid so much as twitched in alarm at what she was about to put into her stomach, she might lose Michel. She closed her mouth, twisted her neck around like an owl, and turned back to him. He wasn't staring like she was. He didn't know why he was there, either. In his mind, that was the real question: What was he doing there with Sara? Fate had gone crazy and thrown him together with the French rose of the university. Maybe he regretted letting her out of the lecture hall that day. The "proper" thing would've been to turn down her invitation since he didn't get why she'd asked to begin with. He didn't want any kind of repayment. And then Sara said, simply, "I'm sorry." And she smiled and kicked her legs in her seat like a little girl. Her exposed skin gleamed whitely. People passing by stared at her, and he worried their gaze would scorch her. He smiled, and the words felt bitter on his tongue: "What are you apologizing for?"

He found the monologue forming rapidly in his mind, without even having to think about it. It flowed off his lips. He was proving to himself that he didn't want her the way other people did. At the very least because desire had turned to stone within him thanks to his abstinence, both voluntary and mandatory. "You're a granddaughter of the Occupation. Look at your green eyes and pale skin. My fight's against *you*." He directed his words at her legs. "I'm not supposed to be here. My place will *never* be here." By "here," he meant at her side. In Sara's ears rose a wave of sound: people at the restaurant, spoons clinking against plates. The smells of koshary and dukka, customers calling out their orders.

The emotion you felt, fear and joy mixed; it was like a girl who's been locked away walking into a garden for the first time. That girl understands people, but flowers and trees are new to her, and she doesn't know what'll happen if she touches them. Will they hurt her? Are they safe?

In that moment, she might've impulsively taken refuge in anyone, anyone but the carpenter across from her. He squeezed his legs together anxiously, as though protecting his manhood. But she smiled like he'd said, "What a wonderful world!" Imagine! A second smile with the same simplicity, Mariam, and it made Michel feel guilty. Reticent. He dusted off his elbows and changed the subject, relaxing his legs a bit. "Lunch is my treat. What do you feel like eating?"

The smallest plate of koshary they had. And a bottle of mineral water. Because Mademoiselle Sara wasn't going to drink from the pitcher like we do. So he ate, and she ate. He laughed, and she laughed. He asked where she lived. Zamalek. He'd have to take her back himself, to make sure she got home safe. How on earth had she gone walking past all the workshops and garages till she found him? He didn't ask, because he didn't want the story to make his blood boil or leave him sad. He paid the bill and went back out into the street with her, walking from Abou Tarek's toward the High Court of Justice. Should he reach out his hand to her? Was it okay for him to touch her? Would Sara even let him? He insisted on keeping her on the inside of the sidewalk, away from the street. He said he'd heard about her from classmates at uni. "What did they say about me?" "That you've got foreign roots and you're engaged to some higher-up in State Security." "Okay, and what about you?" Her eyes were clear and calm when she turned there in the street and asked him that question with all the simplicity in the world. *What about you?* "I sketch out chairs in my mind before I start carving. I'm the best carpenter in the church. That's what they say, anyway. I've been commissioned to supply the cafes in the area. But honestly, I'm tired. Which is a secret; this is the first time I've actually said it out loud."

Then about the piece of land confiscated from his father and uncles. A story that'd made the opposition newspapers the year before. Michel described the smell of blood when the doorman was slaughtered and left there next to the wall as a warning from the big boss.

Anyone who objected would meet the same fate. His father and uncles shut up and decided to compromise, whatever form that took. But he couldn't do it. The result was a blow to the chin. They arrested him without charge. For a month, they kept him in their care.

He laughed. He slapped his right leg and laughed. After the word "care." The slap sounded dull against his flesh. Sara thought the leg must be made of wood. She didn't know if they'd tortured him in prison. Is that what he meant by care? Torture? Maybe they'd cut off his leg. And he'd carved himself a new one. She was afraid to ask. She just smiled.

When he took his pants off in front of her for the first time, she came close and embraced his leg. It wasn't wood. But it was deformed. She enclosed it within her fingers, massaged it, and lowered her ear to it. She could hear the blood pumping. The prison guard was warning him at the top of his voice to keep his nose out of important people's business. *And speak up when you swear to do it, you piece of shit! You filthy bastard!*

His father only resorted to the church to try and find his son after he was dragged away at university and no one knew where he was. The priest got involved, so they released him. His face was intact when he came out. No broken skin, no marks. But he was limping and limping, the way he would the rest of his life. "I wasn't afraid, Father; the blessed tree bears blessed fruit. Right?" The Father had had enough of him. Before Michel disappeared, he predicted it. "You will die for nothing."

Mariam. Sara got home, to their big house in Zamalek. To their marble doorway. She kept walking. He stopped.

It was evening. The security guard noticed the carpenter. Sara couldn't smile at Michel with him there. Between their two bodies, they left enough space for ten people. He was radiant in his rags. Afraid to wave goodbye to her under the security guard's stare. Because at university, Mariam, they were used to people staring; it was a campus of informers. Without further ado, he turned and left. Disappeared into the dusk. She wasn't able to smile. What did you feel, Sara? *Loss, like my mother had launched me out into the world and abandoned me.* The informer was watching her, so she took the elevator to the seventh floor. Michel was the last person she wanted the whole world to meet.

Because your world, Sara, was hardly a pretty poem. Because waiting on the seventh floor when the elevator door opened was the last person you ever wanted God to create. Salah El-Adl. *Even a lamppost would've been kinder than your father, Arwa, or at least less malicious.* There he was, standing on the steps, all puffed up and giving a speech. "The day of Sara's graduation, God willing, will be the day we sign the marriage contract." Despite being loaded, truly la-di-da, Sara's parents were conservative when it came to customs and traditions. And the engagement was to take place as soon as possible. If Sara'd said a single word, it might've changed her fate and Arwa's. And Mariam's, later on. That one word was no.

You were as silent as if they'd swallowed your tongue. You were as ignorant as if they'd colonized your brain cells and looted them. Sara had never considered how unthinking she was. She knew Officer Salah El-Adl loved her, and she didn't care one way or the other. She hadn't thought she was allowed to have an opinion. Then Michel appeared, and the foundations of her world shook. She obeyed her father's order automatically, politely. She stepped forward and greeted the officer. Her eyes fixed on the floor. His eyes on her. As she expected, he caressed the flesh of her hand when he shook it, like he was testing its softness to please himself. The enemy officer. Michel's foil. After Michel had failed to walk her all the way to the door. The spy extraordinaire, elegant in a suit, however casual. The anti-Michel. Salah's body was athletic, stretched taut as a shotgun. He looked like Ahmed Ramzi in old black-and-white movies. Or at least at that moment, in front of the elevator, he looked just as dull. But you preferred Shoukri Sarhan, or even the sickly Abdel Halim Hafez.

She lay on her stomach in the big bed. God will find a solution to this, I know he will, and then I can sleep with Michel. It was the first time you *really wanted* something, and you gave yourself over to it with everything you had. *I can't marry Salah El-Adl. And it's impossible for me to marry Michel.*

When Michel told her, later, "If you think about it, we didn't make a date that day; I didn't ask for a 'secret engagement,' like it says in the Quran," Sara corrected him: "You mean a 'secret arrangement.'" Every morning, she hoped even more that she would never be tied to Salah El-Adl. Impossible. Then she decided to go look for him. The man she'd started seeing in her dreams, standing in front of her, with ten people between them. Staring at her with the gaze of someone who owned nothing but had everything. And, always, Mariam, in her dreams, he turned and walked away.

At the front of the pack of protesters. He raised a hand to his ear. Put the other on his right leg. And he repeated what the angels dictated to him. Immediately, without stopping to understand. "We are slaves to no one and will be inherited no longer." Who did he mean by "we"? His words made the crowd explode. They shouted with him and hauled him onto their shoulders. They ran with him. And they didn't know where to. The boss and the university's security team were no better than rats now. They asked for and received orders. *Open the gates down to the water for them.* Cairo University Bridge. The Nile was a better fit for them. Reminds you of the old king, right? But the sticks went mad, reckless and violent, before the order could be carried out. They pursued them, kissing their backs, hoping to destroy them. The protesters had to drop Michel. His hand was still on his right leg. The only way he managed to escape was to jump into the Nile. That day, he wrote his first message to Sara: "I saw you in every woman I passed in the demonstration; I wanted to die to get away from you."

People thought Michel *had* died, and good riddance. Sara's heart sank into her stomach. She swore she would confess to her father, no matter how he might punish her. She was holding Baudelaire's poems and wearing a sleeveless pink nightgown. "Baba, I don't want to marry Salah El-Adl. I'm in love with someone else." Like she was telling him good morning. He didn't even look up. Sleepily, he responded, "Fine, Sara, now go get some rest." She flew to her room and bounded into bed. *Now, Michel, the world is free!* She wrote to him for the first time: "I didn't go to lectures yesterday, and today my heart almost stopped when I asked what happened at uni. Please tell me you're still alive."

Later, she wedged the note under the door of the workshop, which had been closed for days. She waited at a distance for hours, wrapped in a long, black cloak and veil, unseen by anyone. Hours, days. Till a week had passed. *I was so angry, but I went up to him anyway, and I wanted to slap him. His only response, "I never would've guessed you could write in Arabic. And such pretty handwriting!"* The veiled woman told Michel the carpenter that she wasn't going to marry Salah El-Adl and that her father had agreed she could marry Michel. Even the man she loved didn't take her seriously. It was as though he hadn't heard her. "Look, woman, you're like the Occupation to me; I won't be your slave." She just touched her cheek and smiled. Deep inside, she decided to leave and never come back to him, no matter what happened.

Imagine, even when I was upset with you, I threatened the Nile. I said that if it ever swallowed you, it'd better be ready to swallow me, too.

And I banged my head against the wall and asked it, "What does she want from me; what does she want from Michel?" If Michel the carpenter worshipped you as he worshipped wood, how could the wood live without him? How would his family live?

Sara stopped attending her lectures. At home, she felt true malice for the first time. If he'd been there in front of her, she'd have killed him. Or humiliated him. Carpenter son of carpenters, he ruled over her heart with an iron fist. He might've been out of reach, but being sick wasn't. She lay in bed. Listless. Like her soul had left her. She didn't answer friends' phone calls. She stressed to the servants that they were not to open the door to anyone asking about her, *especially* if they looked poor. The servants didn't really get that. What they did understand was that fever had been making people say strange stuff since the dawn of time. "Yes, Ms. Sara." And Sara said yes to Death with the same obedience and waited for him to obey her. They took her to the hospital with circulatory collapse.

I died, and it was over. And when I opened my eyes, life was like a cloud, and I was floating far above the earth. Far from it all, except the idea that I didn't matter to him. His life didn't have any room in it for the comfort of love. Or the comfort of the pain of love, Arwa. But Salah El-Adl visited me with his servants and his entourage. They turned the hospital upside-down. Baba was so proud that his daughter was the reason for all the hubbub. My last words to them: "I swear to God I am a slave to no one and will be inherited no longer." I tried to raise my arms, but they fell back down beside me. I was weak and abject.

Mariam, what does it mean to be abject?

The doctors lavished attention on the young pasha and revived his future bride. Despite his age, he was the strongest candidate for assistant to the minister of the interior. To Michel: "I decided to write to you when I realized how little you valued me. I'm ready to march with you against the Occupation. Against Al-Azhar. Against the church. Against Russia or America. Even France. Ready for Salah El-Adl to throw me into the gas ovens. For them to take me out to the Sa'id and slaughter me as an adulteress. I'm offering you my whole occupying body so you can enslave it however you like. In any position you like. Will you feel victorious then?"

At the Police Hospital, in a charming family celebration, Ms. Sara El-Marakbi was engaged to the youngest-ever assistant to the minister of the interior, Salah El-Adl.

As you watched the sun set on the world you knew, it was time for you to realize how insignificant you were, to discover that your word had no form or effect; you'd left your poetry books behind forever.

All I wanted from the world was to see you, alive and vital, and to die because of you.

Sara didn't go back to her classes in the spring. They marked her as failed. She was finally on the same level as the carpenter's son.

A yellowed newspaper clipping reached her by way of an impoverished security officer who'd once been an informant. It was in the shape of a boat. Did you know how to make boats, Michel? After all the mental and emotional torture he'd caused, Sara thought about punishing him by sinking the boat. But in the end, she softened, unfolding and reading it.

"#6 Champollion St., 4th floor, next to El Tak'eeba Café, Apartment #8 to the right of the stairs, tomorrow at whatever time works for you, the day after tomorrow at whatever time works for you, or the day after that. The doorman will tell me you're there, and I'll come."

It was this apartment, Mariam!

The morning after she got the message, Sara went to the street and walked in the direction of the workshop. From there, they directed her to #6 Champollion. Like a troll, the doorman appeared from beneath the earth and frightened her. She pretended to be calm. He didn't smirk. He was dark-skinned, short, and thick. He bared his teeth as he spoke, and they were thin like fangs. "Who are you, and what do you want?" "I'm looking for Michel the carpenter." "Are you Sara?" "Yes." Without a word, he approached and handed her a brass key.

The apartment was dark, and Sara didn't look for the light switch. The moment she stepped inside, she sat cross-legged on the green straw rug. She didn't look around. She sat and waited. Seven hours, her mind like a desert. He came in the evening and knocked, gently. She opened the door for him, and he apologized. "I'm sorry, you have the only key." He lit a dim candle, fixing it on a tile that jutted out a little from the others. He went to the meter and reconnected the power. He could see her, then, all of her. He continued his apology. "I was the only one at the workshop. They wanted me to finish three chairs in one day. I didn't sleep at all last night."

She wished he would be less gentle. The gentleness was torture to her. She threw herself against his chest. "I smell like sweat, I'm sorry." "Tell me, please, how did they torture you in prison?"

And then she collapsed. He carried her farther inside. In a later time, you and I, Mariam, would call that room the oboe room. He lowered her back to the earth, laying her down on the same green rug that covered the living room floor. He opened the big window. The view was a void. Michel ran to the kitchen and twisted a knob at the sink, and water gushed out, soaking his olive-green shirt and black pants. He cursed himself and rushed back with a pool of water in his cupped hands, spilling some as he ran, before he made it to Sara. From there to here, here to there, a thousand times over. Finally, Sara woke up. It was as though the wasted water had escaped into her eyes. She rose tearfully and whispered, without raising her arm or her fist, "I swear to God I will be inherited no longer, and I will be no one's slave—except yours."

Later, she wrote, "I was leaning against your chest when I felt you grow hard under my arm, and I smiled and hoped you would never go soft again."

"You were a woman made of wax, and I had never known anything but wood; your body was white wax, with a wing unfurling from each breast."

There were no first caresses then, Mariam. Sara lay back on the floor and spread her legs. Michel entered her, and she felt pain and stifled it. A wooden staff, he slipped into her like a fish into water and swam all the way to her heart. *I refuse to be free of you. My children will never be free of you.* They stayed there half a human day, a full day for the sun or moon. Then they were starving. Spent. Michel's knee was burning; he could feel ants gnawing at him. The prickling didn't stop when they stopped making love, and he complained to Sara, so she began to touch it, the knee of his wooden leg. She enclosed it within her fingers, massaged it, lowered her ear to it. She could hear the blood pumping. The prison guard was warning him at the top of his voice to keep his nose out of important people's business. *And speak up when you swear to do it, you piece of shit! You filthy bastard!*

She started up from where she lay on the floor beside him. Just like you're picturing it, Mariam. If I stood over you, you would see me through the eyes of an ant, and I would be, to you, the terrible Sphinx. Imagine it: your nerves are burning, and despite the fatigue, you're just as turned on as you were at the start. Michel, the man at #6 Champollion Street, needed to get up and straighten his back completely. Then he had to imitate Sara by rotating his legs up and around, as though pedaling a bike. Sara demonstrated the exercise for him in the oboe room that had no oboe. Absorbed in inventing a solution, the two reeds of her thighs shook. Her hair fluttered. She understood nothing about the thing that had just been inside her. The one that objected to her standing there naked and apart. It didn't want a respite.

"Okay, I'll try."

He stood up and began to mimic her. Her eyes lit up. She wanted him to find relief so that she could find it, too. She continued to demonstrate. Her head was turned to the right, where he stood, and her neck muscles started to crack. Michel decided to put an end to this nonsense. "Enough, Sara." An order. Her eyebrows shot up, worried he might be upset again. He faced her. He wrapped his arms around her and lifted her, for a moment, off the ground, then took her hand and placed it low against his body. "You've worn me out, woman!"

She laughed, her entire body shaking. He reached out to run his hands over her, bewildered. She took a step backward, and he gritted his teeth in protest: "What now?" Sara lifted her thigh just enough to squash an ant and threw herself at him. Pain flooded his features, and she felt a malicious joy. She pushed him back down onto the rug, pulling his hair and banging his head against the wall.

Sara didn't tell me, Mariam, how much time passed.

But she told me what Michel saw in his daze, in the fog that spanned Sara's skull. There, into the fog, he advanced.

He saw his own double, a woman named Nousa. Naked. Her skin was pale, and though all that was visible was her back, her paleness shone white like the sun. She looked like the statues of Greek goddesses from long ago, but she was only human, and avenging angels had bound her. Michel had a long beard like Socrates; he gasped for breath in the fog and wanted to know how he would die. He heard her screams as though echoing back to him from the future. Nousa had committed adultery, and there had to be punishment. He made the deal with the angels as quickly as possible: "Leave her alone and take me instead." The throng fell silent. They turned to him, and it became clear that they weren't angels. Faces smiled wickedly. "You want to take her place?"

Socrates felt a fiery prickling sensation in his legs and thought that by dying, he would be freed from the torment in his lower half. In his head, he could still hear her screams in the future, her fear of being slaughtered.

"Yes, I want to take her place."

"You get one request."

"To see her body one last time, from her face to her toes."

Nousa wobbled like a drafting compass with only one leg. Like a mechanical ballerina. Socrates wept. Vomit hot as lava gushed from his mouth, like a volcano he hadn't known was rising inside him. He called out a single name. Sara's. She wasn't around. She'd left the apartment, or his voice would've shattered her. Michel's head fell like an overripe fruit, never harvested, and he lost consciousness.

Sara was at the store down the street. Her heart was dancing circles around itself. Life was more beautiful than poetry. But that was a secret; not everyone knew. You, Sara, had to keep the secret. She picked out bread, tuna, a packet of Nesto cheese, and some water. She collected a bigger haul than her slight arms could carry. Life was beautiful, and the cashier was tapping away at a machine resembling a typewriter when the wooden staff pierced her heart. The first time, it was a light prod. As you might expect, Mariam, Sara smiled to ease the pain from the prod. The cashier saw her smile and thought it strange; he did not smile back. He turned to put the groceries into bags. He didn't know that the piercing sensation had increased and that it was now difficult to breathe. Tears welled up in her eyes for no reason. She snatched a bottle of mineral water from the pile of purchases before running away. Luckily, she'd paid the bill, so the cashier didn't cry thief. When he was sure she was gone and wasn't coming back, he put the purchases back where she'd found them.

How strange, Mariam!

Sara went to the carpentry workshop first. There, she found Michel's father. He was snoring, the newspaper covering his face. She plucked it off, and the man jumped. "Where's Michel?" He snatched it back from her and, half-awake, sent her on her way with the address: #6 Champollion Street.

His words brought her back to herself, and she remembered the rest of the story.

She ran like a woman possessed, her feet pounding up the stairs. The apartment door was still ajar. She was panting when she reached it. She paused for a few seconds before entering. Then she shot through like a bullet. Michel was close to suffocating as the lava blocked his nostrils and spread across his eyelids.

"Michel."

She lifted his head into her lap. She uncapped the water bottle and slowly put it to his mouth. It didn't work like she thought it would. She searched the apartment for something to wipe his chest with and found her red underwear. It occurred to her to call him by her name. So she did. "Sara."

It reverberated in his eardrum. *Sara.*

Michel woke up. He could hardly believe he was still alive. Sara made him a promise. "There's no life for me without you, nothing good in the whole world if we part."

Sara told Salah El-Adl what had happened between her and Michel. She read him the poems by Baudelaire she'd read to herself. The crazy woman, if she could've just made him taste love the way she had, she would've. All she wanted was his unconditional forgiveness and to be released from the engagement. But Salah announced for the room to hear that he would pardon Sara forever on condition that she never go back to Michel. Then Sara's soft voice went sharp over the phone line. She said she would only leave Michel over their dead bodies.

She never imagined that the angel of destiny, standing over her, decided to hang on to that wish for later. If she'd known, maybe she wouldn't have said it. From his position behind the wires and electroshock devices that transformed prisoners into monsters, his voice sounded normal as he said goodbye. The call ended, and she had no choice but to call him back. Just so he could say hello and then laugh when he heard her begging, "Please, Salah, please." He put the phone down but didn't hang up, leaving her on the line to hear a prisoner moaning. Sara swallowed hard and imagined he was a dog. The dog was reveling in her pain. When he picked up again, she would appeal to his chivalry: "I'm sorry I got you into all this; I swear I couldn't help it." The secret of his meteoric rise in the Ministry of the Interior was somehow dishonest; that much was obvious. Salah El-Adl knew Sara better than any other human created by God. He saw her naked before she ever undressed in front of him. He told her so once.

"No, of course. You just surprised me, and I need some time to sort it out."

He got her to stop crying and ask, "What does that mean, Salah?" He wanted Sara to spend the whole night dreaming about the moment she'd be free. Despite her misgivings, she went to bed promising to send him the biggest bouquet of flowers in the world when the sun came up. To any address he liked. On the card, she'd ask him to hand them out to the inmates, flower by flower, to remind them of their loved ones and take their minds off prison. And she would apologize and promise to keep praying that he would meet sitt al-banat, the perfect woman.

When the sun rose, it was Salah who surprised Sara with the biggest bouquet of flowers she'd ever seen. She received it in her nightgown. Barefoot. Thunderstruck. Her eyes were puffy from sleeplessness and tears, and she could barely stop herself from thinking about suicide. She didn't understand and didn't notice the card that fell to the floor when the delivery guy handed her the gift. Without thinking, she carried the bouquet to the bathroom. She put it under the showerhead and turned on the water. For the first time in her life, she wanted to kill flowers.

Her father appeared and asked her what had happened. It felt in that moment like she had no choice but to tell him the truth in the ugliest way possible. "Flowers from Salah El-Adl. I'm drowning them. If you have a problem with that, I'll drown myself, too, and be done with all of you." Sara turned to Michel for help. You could guess as much. Like a rabid dog, she ran to him as he worked in the shop, and he was startled and fell. The wood he was working fell, too, and she grabbed his sleeve, pulling him to her. She told him the story in a minute, the words falling in a rush from her lips like she was possessed. She proposed they run. "What do we have in Egypt? What do you have? You're Christian, and the whole world is churches. Let's leave, let's go to Bavaria, let's make it our promised land. I'll change my name to Arwa, to Nousa, and I'll never need anyone from my family for the rest of my life. If we want to be free, it's our only shot, Michel; under this roof, we'll only ever be slaves."

Sara pointed to the sky with an overly white hand.

She was right. And Michel didn't say no. Even though he felt helpless, like he couldn't leave his family. Even though he worried about the workshop. Even though the idea of dying in a foreign country freaked him out and he wanted to ask his leg how far it could actually carry him, if he really could walk forever. Michel agreed even before answering. The carpenter's son returned to the apartment on Champollion. He prayed and asked the Virgin to guide their steps. When he finished praying, he raised tearful eyes to her. He was upset that Sara had suggested they leave and then walked away so quickly. Spending some time together at the apartment hadn't even crossed her mind. Michel wrote to her: "You could've thought of me as a child craving his mother's breast when he's too ashamed to ask because she's cold and miserable."

Oh, Michel, I wish you were that child. I wish you'd asked.

Don't think for a minute, Mariam, that Michel didn't resist. That Sara didn't resist. Once, she would've been happy for her father to keep her on his pedestal. Beauty, good manners, and a husband from State Security. The straight and narrow. As it was, Sara became a whore in everybody's eyes: her family's, her husband's, her lover's, later on even the doorman's. Sara stopped reading poetry. Obviously. But she wrote letters. Banished books from her sight. But finished her final year of college, got an overall grade of "pass" and her bachelor's degree. She disappointed her professors and all their wishes for a bright future, devoting herself to love, whatever that would mean for her. Devotion is the weakest sort of faith. If she'd had any other way to punish herself, she would've. Life had become, over time, a book in a language that was no longer readable. But it had to be based on something.

She got permission and went to see him. In the doorway of the workshop where he stood tormented. She told him, "I need a break for a month, Michel, and then life will either be ours, or it won't." She endured his snub. She expected it. He pushed her away. She took off the scarf draped over her chest and lifted her sleeveless blouse, standing half-naked in the middle of the street. She meant it as an invitation, knowing he would refuse as a sort of revenge. When he turned away from her and immersed himself in his work, hammering the wood of the chair between his legs, it was like she wasn't there anymore. She wished it was her he was stepping on, that he would hammer a nail into her wrist and see her bleed in front of him. When he said, "I don't want you anymore," she didn't get upset. Her mind summed it all up in three words: *Tomorrow, the revolution.*

But tomorrow was a long way off. Salah El-Adl told her on Day One that staying with him meant Michel would live and that the day she left would be the day he died. He said she was the most delicious woman he'd ever touched, and that with her, he would've liked all of life to be a bed. He caressed her for a year before he finally took her, and still it was painful. Even her vagina pushed him away. She yielded only when he wept in her lap and told her how he tortured his prisoners. Deprived husbands of their wives. He bit her on the neck, in the middle of her chest, and below. The hair stuck between his molars. He was carving out his mark on her, like he was erasing the mark of the man who came before. Then he entered her and cried out in triumph. After he climaxed, he went quiet. He lay across the mattress. The ceiling seemed to close in. He stood up, naked, and begged her in God's name to forgive him all his sins against creation. And from her position, stretched out looking up at him, wounded and pale, she forgave. She covered her breasts with her hands in front of this stranger and repeated, "In God's name, I forgive you for everything except Michel." She insisted. "The Copt. You stole everything from him. Give me back to him, and God will forgive you."

But Salah El-Adl, as you can imagine, Mariam, did not forgive. She remained there, trapped between his legs, delirious. "Take me back to Michel." Her head would peer out between the ribs of his athletic frame, and she would groan. She fainted sometimes, and raved. He was the bulldozer uprooting flowers and throwing them in God's face. In her imagination, she tried to run from the torture, fleeing into the arms of a spellbound lover. Imagination was rarely good enough.

Michel, meanwhile, was trapped inside the apartment on Champollion Street. For years, he wouldn't talk to her and only softened in that last year, the year of his resurrection and death. He told me the story himself, one I already knew. After their quarrel, he started fixing up the apartment. A thousand trees' worth of wood is scattered inside; he built furniture for every room. He yanked up the straw rug, remembering them there together. Then he regretted it and decided that everything he made for the apartment would be done for one person. Michel was a novice in bed and in choosing paint colors: a faded pink wardrobe for Michel's childhood clothes because that child had never met Sara or fallen in love. He made the bedroom door the same color as the light switch, the color of the Nile he'd once thrown himself into. The wood was warped, and he didn't straighten it out. He worked stubbornly at a simple table, a crooked one he used to fill the empty space and prove he could work miracles without her. He wasn't interested in completeness. He might even have sought out lack. Later, whenever Sara opened the door, she hit that table. And when Mariam runs in our play, she hits it, too. Here, in the middle of the ceiling, an old lamp throwing all its light on the floor, trailing there like an old caveman's beard. Sometimes it was the only source of light in the apartment.

In the oboe room, Michel made do with building bookshelves that never saw a book during his lifetime. In front of them, he left space for Sara to draw. He removed the handles of the doors and windows and fashioned new ones out of slivers of wood that were thin, like him, fit for just one person's hand. For the kitchen, he chose deep, dusky colors, and he decorated the balcony with fresh garlic. He painted the bathroom ceiling by hand, weeping on the iron ladder, and in the seventh week after they parted, Michel collapsed from grief.

And Mama was pregnant.

The flesh of the apartment is exposed now, Mariam. You can tell. It's really strange. It's gone all damp and sticks to the skin. If you close your eyes, you can hear the sound. It's impossible not to dream here. If you fall asleep in its darkness, the place protects you from soldiers and from pointless death. The day I visited it, I knew I would never forget it. But I lied to myself. I tried to gain some distance, but it only pulled me deeper in. I realized it was fate when the revolution broke out and I saw the crowds creeping onto screens that resounded with their chants. I played the apartment a song I learned on the oboe. A plaint I play in the squares over there, among foreigners. It moves them when they hear it, and they clap. They can see all the way to the seven heavens, feeling something without knowing what it is. Music can bring a home to life anywhere in the world. . . . It can save it the way it saved me. I pity you, my love. From here on out, all the strangeness of the apartment on Champollion Street is yours, too. You don't have a choice, and you won't be able to ask for help. To tell anyone or complain. From now on, you'll never ask what time it is. Or what day it is.

Do you understand, Mariam?

Mariam. If you'd seen the figure I cut arriving at the Cairo airport that day, you'd have been put off by me, even more than you were later, in the metro. Or maybe you'd have smiled and held on to your innocence, in spite of everything. Years ago, I boarded a Lufthansa jet determined never to come back, but I did come back, a German passport in my pocket. Since the revolution broke out last January, I've been drawn more than ever to everything Egypt-related. I know the country's been sensitized against foreigners the way I'm so sensitive to a cold that it robs me of my voice. At this point, I look like a foreigner. I *am* a foreigner. And whether I expected it or not, I had to justify my reasons for coming back to every officer, soldier, and janitor I saw, to a never-ending line of humans, waiting for them to ask so I could answer—even if I didn't know what to say. I returned because I couldn't *not*. Believe me when I say I didn't know why I came back till I saw you in the metro and sat down beside you: maybe that's why I upset you, so I'd have to make up with you. In the short arrivals line beside the long departures line, I came up with my final answer: in English and without batting an eyelash, I would say, "Work." The customs officer looked at me with suspicion and asked carefully, "Why are you coming here now, Ma'am?" And I said, "Work" with all the self-importance I could muster. Then, light-fingered, I plucked up my passport from the window between us, and he didn't dare object because I raised my eyes to the ceiling like, *Don't make me get the ambassador*. Obviously I was a little scared at first that the game of chicken would come back to bite me in the ass. I didn't fly all the way here so they could throw me in prison. He could've tossed me in a corner, confiscated my stuff, or at least asked me about the nature of my work in Egypt.

And at that point, what would I have said? Especially since I hadn't met you yet, and didn't know I was about to meet you. Especially since they would never in their lives accept us. But no need. I hoisted the oboe case onto my shoulder and grabbed the handle of the bag I dragged over the wide airport floor, like nothing had happened, or would happen, while on the inside I chanted at them: *LIARS, sons of DOGS, LIARS, sons of DOGS!* Soon I would realize that all I had were those chants. But first I had to get out of this official building, all safe and cold. It's hard, Mariam. Hard to pretend like, after all the distance, returning doesn't hurt the way it hurts being gone, or worse. I only came back because ever since I left, I'd been pulled back toward the Nile by my hamstrings. The image might make you giggle, but the truth is that when I left, I walked away and kept on walking.

What was I like? It's like I was Eve, the first woman created by our Lord in between repeated copies of Adam. Eve, created by the Lord as Adam slept, after hunger and thirst. Mouths stretched wide in a strange smile I couldn't explain: malicious joy or ignorance? A deceitful smile I forced myself to be patient with as I faced Cairo, Cairo whose desolation would attack unexpectedly in winter and summer, every time I neglected my health because of music, because of love or even grief. I was expecting to get sick that day. My truth is that my body's punishing me because I brought it to hell, to a place where men's eyes crack like whips across my back. I knew the consequences, Mariam.

I was gloomy and didn't understand why people dispersed the way they did around me, following me. Maybe they wanted to harass me, or, like me, they were arriving from a long trip with their mouths hanging open and their memories erased, empty. They nearly triggered my anger, which could've swallowed the airport, almost forced me to say, *I don't care what you think, I'm no Eve*, when I heard the word "Limousine?" and turned toward its source. I was surprised by the elderly driver who'd pronounced it with the smile of someone whose country wasn't in full revolution, a perfectly normal person who was speaking to me in the language of signs because I was a foreigner, pointing at his white sedan, a Shahin. Limousine? It'd been years since I'd seen one of these; I was close to nostalgia and on the brink of dissolving into tears like a little kid. I ignored the hollers of the other drivers and spoke only to him: "Yes, to Champollion Street downtown, by Koshary Abou Tarek—do you know it?" The man laughed, a disappointed laugh, and that's when the officers noticed me, stopped speaking, and raised their eyebrows in disapproval, as though I'd committed some public indecency by speaking Arabic.

No one expected me to speak Arabic, and I could've gone back to the palace over there in Masaken El Dobat, El Remaya. I could've chosen not to keep torturing myself with all the old methods of torture rolled into one big weapon: Egypt, the apartment on Champollion, the revolution, the oboe. I could've lured you to a place near yours where it would be easy for your grandmother to find us, or imagine that she could, and where it would be easy for you to feel at home. But my real home, my *real* home is here, where the dust nestles and darkness floods the space, and I would never forgive myself if I seduced you anywhere else.

I didn't ask You for justice; I never asked You for justice. What could I possibly want from it?

You were in the street, Mariam, and you weren't, and I was in the street, and we were on the verge of meeting when we met. I wanted to do what I'd abandoned my life to do, what I'd learned over the years to say in the most tender way possible, in the most violent way possible, with music. I hadn't cleaned this apartment because when I arrived, I was driven back out like a bullet from a gun, afraid that for some reason it would ricochet.

I didn't look around when I got out of the taxi, and I didn't think about the people talking and playing backgammon in cafes because they weren't, couldn't be, the same ones I'd left sitting there. I took the bag and oboe and started to climb the stairs, ignoring the shocked doorman as he called out offering his help and, later, his wife's help. I recoiled in disgust and irritation at the door and hissed to shoo him away the way you'd shoo a dog: "Hshhhhhh." I'll never forget what he did to us. He finally left me alone as I put the brass key in the old lock. It turned and then snapped, simply, as though it had been waiting for ages to snap, and the door opened onto total darkness. I stepped across the threshold and invited the spirits to pass through me; the familiar wind was the same, and I smiled. I repressed the urge to cry or to reproach. *You told Arwa to leave, Sara, and not to come back. Do you still remember, Sara, what Arwa was like?* I left my things in the living room, lit a candle, and flipped the light switch; the lamp in the bedroom came on, and with its light I recalled my astonishment when I discovered my sense of hearing for the first time, as though I'd suddenly received a gift. As soon as the switch slipped into place, I could clearly hear the screams, cries for help, laughter, and death rattles coming from Tahrir Square, the Cabinet building, and Mohammed Mahmoud Street, as though the noises had gathered themselves together and were marching in formation toward my apartment on Champollion. Unmistakable noises approaching, like drums and the stomping of conscripted soldiers. I didn't pull the deadbolt behind me. This is what I'd come for, how I wanted to torture myself. I greeted the picture of the Virgin Mary in the studio, or the oboe room, as we call it. I had the oboe with me in its case, and I took the stairs back down, racing the fever that forced itself from my forehead. People were shivering, and I was about to melt out of my skin. The same look of disapproval I'd gotten from the officers at the airport, that malicious glee. I found myself at the beginning of Mahmoud Bassiouny Street without knowing how I got there, and it suddenly occurred to me to go back and take the metro, to sing underground to the people who were afraid. To make them less afraid.

If all I'd been doing was looking for you, things would've changed. I wouldn't have come back and seen you, and you wouldn't have called out to me, either, or given me the ticket, my ticket to come home to you. A few minutes before you appeared, I was scanning the length and breadth of Champollion Street at roughly the hour I would see you the next day, still not knowing how I'd gotten there. I studied the geography of the area as I'd seen it online. I spotted the famous El Tak'eeba Café, a few tables set out and the atmosphere reeking of caution accompanied by a desire to prove it wrong, to spread the illusion that life was danger-free. I promised myself water and coffee and anise tea in the open air as a reward if I did my job. I bought the metro ticket from Gamal Abdel Nasser station, repeating the directions to myself out loud. Compared to German lines, they were a piece of cake. I smiled, feeling nostalgic. In my mind, I transcribed the names of the presidents: Gamal Abdel Nasser, Anwar Sadat, Mohamed Naguib, even Mubarak. To those presidents, as well as the old women, the men in galabeyas, and the shy girls in hijab—I was the foreign devil speaking to itself in Arabic, the devil whose thoughts they couldn't read, and who they wouldn't be able to understand even if they did. They watched me as I walked into the metro car that stopped right in front of me, the first car the arrow pointed to.

At the root of it, artists make art to express what scares people within themselves, and I had to figure out what I was going to say to this feeling. There were women and men in the metro car, their necks bowed. It was depressing seeing them like that. I'd expected it, but seeing is different than hearing, and all that was left was for me to sit at their feet and beg them to give up their fear in the tense landscape of the train's movement. Most of that sadness was beyond me; I doubted my personal issues could compete with theirs. I'd traveled, learned, loved, seen . . . I'd found myself, Mariam, and I put my hand to my head and tried not to imagine what came next. The constant rocking helped shake the caution from my skin, and then the little kid came up to me. He couldn't have been more than five, and he was wearing a white Zamalek football jersey. He was the only person who smiled and waved at me. It felt like Michel was standing there with me and encouraging me, and I told myself that meant Sara was there, too. She had to be here with me, putting her hand on my shoulder. I got up without grasping the pole and played.

I swear by Mariam that the world went quiet for a long, long moment because of me, and this moment unfurled inside me like a river with birds chirping on its banks, a river that was clear and unpolluted by hatred.

It was the best signal I'd ever received to keep playing. I put the reed between my lips and blew, though I didn't know what I was playing or for who. I was answering the oral question on the exam I lived out in my dreams, as it came to me, and I found myself playing the part of the swan in a symphony by the Greek composer Eleni Karaindrou, the solitary, plaintive swan whose name is oboe. That moment would've become a whole new life, I swear, a recompense, if not for the soldier's skinny fingers cutting it off before it started, digging into my shoulder bone. I was in pain, but I ignored him and kept going, tried to keep going. I saw them dispersing the river, I saw the birds flying away. I kept going till he got bored and angry and decided to take my oboe, at which point the playing turned into screaming.

I looked for you with the same intensity as you looked for me, and that's the only explanation for why we met. When I play, I lose track of my body, Mariam, my whole body, and when I make love, I reclaim it with you completely. I spend my life going back and forth. When they took me by surprise, I was playing. I closed my eyes and propelled myself backward, pushed with all my futile energy. I stepped on feet I'd just been begging at. I let myself fall and felt splitting pain as I hit the barrier, opened my eyes and came crashing back into my body. I was forced to see the scene play out. The people I was performing for didn't intervene, and I didn't see the kid. The doors of the metro car opened wide at the station for soldiers and more soldiers, under orders from the officer, who pointed in my direction, like I was more than Arwa, like I was a multitude of frightening people. I wasn't afraid, Mariam, but in the blink of an eye, the black uniforms and body armor had surrounded me, cutting off my fire and oxygen, so the playing stopped. All I could do was hold on to my only weapon and brandish it in their faces, the oboe like a drawn sword because the oboe was hurting them, because they were terrified of it. They ordered me in the megaphone: "Drop that thing and get out."

I don't know how I got out, but I didn't give up the oboe. Don't know how I made it into the open air. They must've dragged me there, and they must've beaten me. I remember screaming, unleashing all my hatred for Egypt into their faces, at their weapons, and over their helmets. I found myself singing the refrain that had begun in my head at the airport, but without a tune: "LIARS, sons of DOGS, LIARS, sons of DOGS," over and over, and sins heaped on sins, I hurt everyone I could reach.

The officer wanted to put an end to the skirmish, so he broke through my rage and grabbed my neck to strangle me before recoiling involuntarily, startled by the heat emanating from my body, like he'd touched an exposed electrical wire. They backed away from me like I was some supernatural being or devil. It was Baba's prophecy for me. My German passport then freed me from the rest of the procedure once and for all and restored the metro line to its former calm. The people were saying, "Even in the metro, you can't leave us alone." I read the sign for the metro station, "Cairo University," and later learned that I was spared what another girl in the square wasn't. Sitt al-Banat, the Girl in the Blue Bra. There were people watching what happened to her on their mobile screens, and there you were on the station platform, your hair pulled into a crooked ponytail. You were staring into space and smiling to yourself. You didn't know you were smiling to yourself, and nobody sitting nearby pointed it out.

I knew I'd meet you one day, and that you would love me, however silly the idea seemed to you at first. In the past, when Salah shamed Mama for having me, she would say, "Arwa is sitt al-banat. She's perfect." And then she would smile at me like she smiled at no one else, not even Michel. She put her whole heart into that smile, the way you smile at me when I touch you down there and tell you it's as lovely and pale as a dream. You smile with your whole heart, like we're the only two people alive. Arwa, sitt al-banat—it meant I was older than my age, a grown-up woman in a kid's body, a description that made Salah curse me and correct it: No, I was a full-on devil in a kid's body. They were each half right. I wasn't sad. The older I got and the more I understood, the more the reasons for my sadness vanished. When I was little, I never felt strange, like an outsider. When I went off to school, out of the whole world, I thought only of Mama. I knew instinctively that I was why she stayed in that palace . . . I mean, I welcomed you here, Mariam, into this little apartment, but back then we lived in a palace of pure gold, a real one in the middle of a forest on the outskirts of Giza, a neighborhood called El Remaya. Masaken El Dobat—I know the name means something to you.

The palace was protected by soldiers on horseback, and at night they bolted the doors to lock us in. It's where I became intimate with everything kids my age feared: silver wolves, red owls, creatures locked in the palace with us, drained of blood and cast at Baba's command from the most precious metals. At first I thought that Baba was God and our handful of servants were angels. They didn't have the right to time off, never got sick, and were always stoically silent—but angels are kind, and the servants weren't. They relayed every whisper of ours to Baba, especially Mama's: when she laughed, when she cried, when she sat down to write. I don't remember being born, Mariam, but I woke up one day and found myself there, sitting on the ground, my back stiff and my head nodding onto my chest. I didn't try to go back because my memory didn't offer up an alternate life. Then Sara called to me, and I felt better. She took me with her into the white bathroom, the only corner of the palace with no decorations or guards, without any statues groaning in it. Sara stepped out of her slippers in front of me and climbed into the bathtub. I saw her whole body and couldn't believe it, but then I believed and believed. I was amazed when I climbed up with her and she hugged me and sang me a song in French, "Et si tu n'existais pas" . . . She received the first shock of cold water in my place as the heater warmed up, and she lathered me in jasmine soap. Time passed as she scrubbed; jasmine was her favorite scent, and now it's mine. Sara was the first woman in my life.

Then I started school and left her alone at the gates of the forest, getting ready to go back to Michel on Champollion Street after so many years of restraint. She said she was never coming back to Masaken El Dobat, not this time, no matter what. I knew I was why she'd stayed. I knew it but couldn't translate it into words. Me leaving for school meant she would leave, too. Once I was gone, there would be nothing left for her in the palace. For years, she'd written letters to her beloved and sent them out at dawn with the soldiers who came to do our bidding. Whether Michel really received them or Baba did, Mama never stopped dreaming, never stopped waiting by the phone. A few times, she'd gone out and come back before sunset. But now, she could finally go to him herself and give the ink and paper a break. I rode to my school in Zamalek in the car with its tinted windows and private driver, leaving Mama waving goodbye to me like they do in the movies. Ever since I was born, Mariam, I knew that Sara's real home was the Champollion Street apartment. It was just a matter of time before she moved. I kept waving to her till she disappeared and I reached the school gate. I stood in line with the other students like they told me to, and the music started the way it has every day in schools since the dawn of creation, followed by the salute to the flag and the school anthem. The chaos was more than I could bear. I got dizzy and collapsed, and they took me back to a palace where Mama wasn't.

I wondered every day if there would be light at the end of the tunnel—would you be there? Every day I asked, and the question was different, but the meaning was the same. Assuming you didn't know yourself then, would it have been right for you to know me? You poured out all your past life there on the metro tracks where butterflies and mice get crushed when they lose their way. You poured it out and asked me to call and seduce you. Nothing I did was spontaneous, Mariam, but when I was very little, I had no idea how it would all happen. I didn't know that—for you—I would finish the song that got interrupted in the metro, or that I would forget the other people there without worrying about consequences.

At bedtime, when I was small, I would touch her hand with one of mine and press my head into the pillow with the other, then tell her what I could hear happening under the wooden floorboards beneath my bed. Baba wasn't Baba at first. In the basement was the man with the hungry dogs, the rare weapons, the depressed falcons. On the nights he took other women with him, at the happy times of night, she would bury her nose in my neck, and I would stick my earlobe to her flesh. I could hear the blood rushing in her veins and tried to count her heartbeats, but I always got lost and started over. I got to know the world by hearing first, Mariam.

I told Sara I was scared I was turning into a devil, like Salah El-Adl said, because I couldn't possibly be turning into a second King Sulaiman, who could hear djinn and speak to animals, and might've heard ants crawling one story down. Me, I needed an explanation for all the noises. I was on my guard for long days so Salah El-Adl wouldn't notice me, and I imagined people could tell the real size of my ears and somehow knew I didn't get cold in winter like other kids. He's the one who found out how warm I ran and shamed me with it, and shamed Mama, and she answered: "My Arwa is sitt al-banat." Who exactly was Salah El-Adl, Mariam? You can't exactly say he was my father. His throne was underground, and sometimes he liked to sleep there. I knew exactly where the basement was: it was the rectangle just under my bed. After Sara left, I could hear his heart beating loudly, like a warning, and I didn't want to hear it. Sometimes I thought he was a musical instrument enchanted to make the sounds of all the other instruments and that my senses were sharper because he was so awful. He wept and groveled, and I heard him call out women's names I'd never heard in my life: Fawzia, Seham, Nimat. He inevitably made it to Sara's name and would wax eloquent, asking her once to forgive him and to translate his poems into French, and then he would love her. His voice was like nails against the wall and the door of my room, his secret that I kept and hid from everyone, even him. I heard prisoners asking him for pardons as he sniggered. Everything that went on in his head, Mariam, I heard; every day, I touched my ears and was afraid that Salah El-Adl might be right—and if so, what kind of life could I have? For a long time, I wondered if I was somehow eavesdropping on his nightmares—maybe I really did come from Satan.

But people didn't see what I saw. Mama kept saying I was older than my actual age, that I was a woman in a kid's body. Then Salah would shame Mama for having me, and she would kiss me and sing out, "Arwa is sitt al-banat!" I didn't have any friends, obviously, just the sparrows and the pigeons in the trees, creatures in love with running away from me—from humans in general, and unfortunately I actually was human. When was I ever a child, Mariam? When were you?

One day, I went up to the school building like the other students and hesitated at the classroom door. Suddenly, I jumped up onto the wall between the grounds and the staircase, took off my uniform and then my underclothes, and threw them into the stairwell behind me. What was the plan? I wasn't sure, but I tried not to let my legs tremble because if they trembled, I'd fall off the wall and get all bloody. When I relaxed a little, I opened up my arms like I wanted to hug someone and spread my legs wide.

Imagine the scene I made, Mariam.

I wanted the girls—and only the girls—to come closer and copy me. I called them excitedly, "Come on! Come here!" When they seemed frightened, I patted the wall and dusted it off, leaving them the option to sit or stand, and I imitated the chirping of birds to entice them. And yes, Mariam, the eyes around me began glinting merrily even though we all knew this wouldn't last. The boys whistled from the far-off corners but were too afraid to get closer because I threatened them and hissed to shoo them away. Every time I got close to falling, I steadied myself with my arms and spread myself out a little farther. One girl responded to my invitation and began to peel herself bare in front of everyone: nannies and little boys, walls and floor tiles, and the school bell hanging from the ceiling. She was a teenager and older than me. One truth was that I'd never laid eyes on her before, and another truth was that when I discovered her, life suddenly looked different. I remember her now the way I remember my own face as a kid, reflected back to me in the mirror: loud and clear, and nothing can ruin it. The girl came up to me in slow motion as she stripped off everything covering her body, a happy turmoil of emotions. I bit back my breath like a drowning woman as I saw and enjoyed the sight, a dizzy sensation reaching my brain and starting to melt it. I couldn't feel my body anymore, Mariam. I stared and stared, and my heart was ripped through my ribs, and my eyes almost jumped out of their sockets. My senses, tormented by hearing both what I was meant to hear and what I wasn't, felt like they were being grilled over charcoal. I saw my body from above, like the angels, like the dead, and I ached for the exultation that reached me before it was too late. At first, I wanted to hug her, and I could hear voices rising toward us on the stairs and the shouts as she faltered between me and their threats. She looked at me accusingly, and I smiled because what I'd seen was enough for me. She was reproaching me, but for what? I didn't know—maybe for things I wouldn't do till later. I didn't ask anyone to intervene, of course, but they volunteered themselves and pulled me down from there by force. They took the other girl down with the same violence. The difference was that I didn't respond to the punishment they wanted to impose on me, but she responded at once and cried and groveled. They dragged me to the principal's office; they wiped the floor with me, and I didn't even care. The image went away when they covered me up in a green cleaning lady's uniform. They dressed me in it, and my appearance became strange. I had no sense of my own dimensions in it, but that didn't bother me. I was still drunk with ecstasy. For the whole school day, they kept me locked in the fancy office, so I stayed there with them, reliving the scene moment by moment, leaving them behind while I entered the temple, her body, getting lost in it. That evening, Salah El-Adl arrived and saw me in the green uniform, so he brandished his gun at them, cursed, and spat, and later on, they said I was rebelling against his authority.

I swear, Mariam, I didn't even know Salah El-Adl well enough then to rebel like that. I remember how, in the wild noir thriller I apparently starred in that day, all the pigeons suddenly took flight, and I remember my painful search for her every morning after that. She became my purpose in going to school, but as you can imagine, she never crossed paths with me again.

Mariam, that was the first revolution in my life that they suppressed.

In Sara's absence, I lived alone, the days in an unbroken string with the nights. I could go seven days without sleeping, and all I had left was to leave, to go anywhere. The apartment on Champollion Street was as firmly rooted in my mind as the Sphinx, which was clearly visible if I opened Mama's bedroom window and looked. I called for my suitcases from the basement and decided to get all my stuff together, my pictures with darling Sara: her looking feebly at the camera the day I was born, during the difficult days after that, the days she wrote letters to herself in eloquent French to ease the pain, chronicling her life in the language no one else would understand.

Once Sara called me in the middle of the night and said, "I bought you classical music records—all of them!" Then her laughter rang out over the phone. Michel was with her, of course, maybe they were lying together in bed like we are now, his thigh draped over her leg the way mine's draped over yours, and her sweet voice sang out, "I bought you all the classical music records, Arwa."

Michel was the one who came to my school in secret and left the music for me by the Egyptian flag that flew on the rooftop farthest from view. The records were in a black garbage bag; I grabbed it when no one was watching and left school early.

For days, I sat on the ground, naked, the way I liked, scratching my yearning ears against the metal of the huge black headphones, searching for the miracle, the voice of the miracle. Where was it coming from? The music was falling from the ceiling and coming out of the walls, bouncing in the air, Mariam. I was too young to name it, in human words, at least, but in my heart it had a name, and it found its way to me. At that blessed hour, music crept into a heart that couldn't resist it and announced that the two of them were now one. It was obvious: when music found its way to me, it gave my gift meaning. I believed little by little, over time, and only preached the faith in the German language years later. The door closing behind us meant that there was more in that room than me. I wasn't alone and never would be, and the melody followed, like flying angels throwing grains of wheat to the birds, not stopping for even a second for me to touch them or the birds. For weeks, months, and years, I went from record to record, as infatuated with them as if they were women.

In Munich, I learned love and music, and I learned myself.

Six months after Sara died, I went to Munich. I picked Germany to get away from Arabic, English, and French. Emigrating was all I needed to come back to life. In the last days, before she finally left her body behind, she said to me, "Get out of Egypt, like we should've gotten out together." Sara died in a desolate villa in Masaken El Dobat in El Remaya that was all of Egypt to me because I'd listened to her when she told me, "If you leave the palace, your father will haunt us forever, even after death. Salah could never bear to lose you." And though I listened to her and Michel on Champollion when they told me it would be better for everyone if I went back, and I *did* go back, Baba still took out his misery on us.

All the days led up to that fateful day, Mariam. Sara was waiting for me in front of my school, standing there all skinny and awkward, the whiteness of her legs peeking out from her navy skirt. She wasn't wearing stockings under the skirt. It was bitterly cold, but she was wearing a cream-colored strappy top and covering her arms with just a white shawl. I was sure her limbs had gone totally numb. We sent the private driver away. She and I, my empty school bag, and my water canteen wouldn't be going back to Masaken El Dobat. We walked from Zamalek to Champollion Street downtown, and Sara squeezed my hand and blushed for the thousandth time. "Are you sure you want to see him?" I could see the redness in her left cheek and feel the color in her voice, so I warmed to her and teased her, "Sara looks like a rose." I sang some Umm Kalthoum to embarrass her more: "Ha'ablo bokra wa ba'd bokra." *I'll meet him tomorrow and the day after.* It was winter then, too, I could see as clearly as I see you, with no sun to tire us out and no rain. Sara said the weather was perfect for me, so I wouldn't get sick, and I corrected her: the weather was perfect for love, for getting love back. I'd missed my real father so much, I said. It was November. I saw the doorman in his dirty galabeya for the first time, and he saw us, turning up his nose and asking God's forgiveness. We left him behind and hurried upstairs. The first time I entered the apartment on Champollion Street, I could feel Sara's heart beating in my chest, like it might stop, like I was her and Michel was *my* beloved, or like his face was the face of the girl who'd disappeared from the schoolyard forever. Sara wasn't complete till that day, and she struggled to breathe evenly in my presence. You were so eager to embrace the apartment and its inhabitant, Sara. You'd never lived in a home; before this, they'd all just been waystations. I inherited that from you. You tilted your face upward, trying to catch a whiff of Michel's scent, and he heard us on the stairs and opened the door before we could ring the bell. The first thing he did was apologize. "I'm sorry, Arwa, the bell hasn't worked for a long time. Mama knows that."

Then he pulled me into a hug, ignoring her. I smelled his sweat, and an abrupt surge of jealousy swept through me. It melted away when he told me she'd mentioned to him how much I loved music. We sat down, and he pulled a harmonica out of his pocket, a simple instrument the size of a kid's palm, its sound like newborn birds. Michel breathed his soul into it, and a tune emerged that was trying and failing to be the anthem we sang in the morning at school. I decided to correct him and took the instrument and improvised the right melody. Michel leaned back into the living room chair you first sat on. He was drawn to me, completely forgetting Sara was there. He saw her in me, and I saw her in his eyes as they sparkled. He framed me in the pretend camera of his brown hands and then winked and said, "What a beauty you are, Arwa. You'll drive men crazy."

And Sara laughed.

Sara died slowly, in stages. Even her peaceful sleep in the coffin was taken for granted. I'd decided to stay there and play the harmonica every day at sunset from the window overlooking El Tak'eeba, forgetting the past, but Michel convinced me to go back to Masaken El Dobat so that Baba's misery couldn't touch us. I would visit them every so often and sit in the window to play then. I listened to Michel and left, so I didn't see it when he died. Like you, but before you, Mariam, I didn't believe what happened. Baba's soldiers burst into the apartment, and Mama was so terrified that she fainted. They tied a rope around Michel's neck, and time passed as they mocked him, yanking him around as he shouted at them in fear. Then, in the space of a breath, they dragged him to the window in the oboe room and threw him from the fourth floor—the fourth floor, Mariam. Michel landed next to the café. He landed on his nose, and his body convulsed like a slaughtered chicken until the ambulance got there. He lay in the dust as Sara rushed tripping down the stairs. At the end of the nightmare was Michel. She put one hand in his and with the other stroked his hair as she told him he was only a little broken. "You're only a little broken, Michel; you'll live." Sara was in shock. She couldn't believe the soldiers had done what they'd done and then calmly revived her to say her goodbyes. Was that another order from my father? My mother was convinced that, to them, we were nothing but insects. Michel could hear her voice but not see her, repeating "Sara, Sara" as the café patrons gathered around him, urging him to recite al-shahada. He kept tugging at the rope still tied around his neck, choking him, but Michel would never utter another word ever again. The paramedics arrived and isolated him from her, as if they knew in advance what to do. They covered his body with a black garbage bag. Maybe Michel didn't know he'd died, maybe he would've kept fighting, but the slender male nurse leaned over him and whispered, "You're dead," so he stopped trying.

They took him away and left Sara there on the ground, greedily filling her mouth, nose, and chest with the dirt he'd bled on. The dirt kept trickling away. I don't know, Mariam, how she got to the phone, or how she made it through her usual greeting before telling me, before we got cut off.

"Arwa, they threw Michel in the trash."

Who would I tell if not you?

When I got to Munich, I saw the world through the plane window before going down the iron stairs. It was very dark and cold, and it was raining like it hadn't rained in ages, for reasons it wouldn't tell.

On that first long trip, I stacked two suitcases on top of each other like I'd seen practiced travelers do, and I staggered over to a young female officer who stamped my passport and smiled. "Welcome to München." I got lost in the underground twists and turns leading to the metro station and was exhausted. I'd insisted on creating a homeland for myself that wasn't Egypt, and I was determined enough to move abroad and absorb all the symbols on the signs, even if they all looked the same to me. I tried to memorize the pronunciation of the metro stations as the announcer called out the stops. Back then, Arabic was still my reference point. I hadn't become fluent in German yet. From the train windows, I could see green on both sides and the kind of pretty little houses we drew in school, convinced the only place they existed was on paper. Within two hours of discovering this new, German world, I reached the Isar, the long river that wends its way tirelessly through Munich. I was in Bavaria, the land Mama had longed for before me and died still longing for, and the hotel where I'd reserved a room was exactly fifty steps from the river. I got out of the taxi and went in with my passport to fill out the form with my name, country, length of stay, and purpose of stay, and feeling hopeful, I wrote a single word in the blank for "length of stay": forever. With the same simplicity, I listened to the instructions regarding breakfast and the phone number for the reception desk in case of emergency, both of which I forgot before I reached the elevator. There I found a young couple speaking broken English. She had pale lips and short blonde hair blanketing her skin like a lioness, and he had the innocent face of a teenager. They sounded angry, then appeasing, and then she proposed a very specific plan: he would sleep with her next to the river, outside in the cold, and she wanted to come three times.

You're laughing, Mariam? Oh, you should've seen it . . . I threw my stuff down in my room without shutting the door behind me. I listened to the little voice in my head whispering that I should spy on them. The boy started trying to bargain with her: "*Or* what if we stay at the hotel instead, but you come ten times?" She yelled and threatened him till he granted her wish, which was what I wanted, too. I slipped down the stairs after them, jumping lightly, my feet barely touching the ground. I was basically flying. The key was in one pocket, and I clenched a sweaty hand in the other. I wasn't gonna miss this. They'd stolen me away without an umbrella, and I was soaked. Meanwhile, they warmed themselves with kisses every few steps.

That's lovers' justice for you.

Near the bridge was a staircase carved from the rock, making me think how strong the sculptors must have been, and the Isar left droplets on both sides, which forced us to descend with caution. I hung back a little and listened to them, oblivious to my presence and dazed with love. The girl suddenly stopped and shouted, "Son of a bitch, rougher!" and then kept going down, closer to the river. She was punishing him for being so shy in front of nature, and he slapped her lightly because he didn't want to go any farther. For the first time since the fight started, he was decisive and said, "Here." *Here* was the hollow of a tree, the squirrel that lived in it having woken up at all the noise and fled, panicked. They entered its narrow hollow and curled into each other, lost to the world, quivering and shuddering twenty times over. I left them there and continued the walk down to the river, freeing my hand from my pocket and letting it breathe, unintentionally performing what you would call the sign of the cross. I wanted the rain to enter my black heart and for the river to pass by and sweep it clean.

I was a different woman when I went back to the hotel, like I was the one the lover had slept with, like I was the one who'd slept with her. I was both the lover and the beloved. I don't know how many times it happened, or if she was satisfied. I threw myself on the bed and sank into sleep, and when I woke up to change my clothes from the night before, I remembered dreaming about Sara and Michel making love in the squirrel's hollow, intertwined, lost to the world, cold and panting with the fever of love. They noticed the baby animal standing watching them with a harmonica in its pocket. They laughed for a few seconds, then went down to the river to hide their nakedness.

Noémie is the one who transformed the harmonica into an oboe.

What happened is this: I went out that night and walked along the river, going wherever it led me, till I found myself in front of a cultural building with a church behind it. I was drawn toward it as the church bells rang for prayer. In the sudden pause when they stopped, I heard loud music calling me from deep inside the building, so I pushed open the door and went in. The darkness was meant to make the stages look dignified, with a simple light casting a dancing rainbow of colors over them. The Moroccan rai they were playing was the icing on the cake, all madness and wild human energy. Then, Mariam, my gaze fell on her. I saw Noémie.

The music was like a ring of fire, and she was in the middle of the ring, a light that everyone was meant to see, but luckily, only I could. An oboe player encircled by the saxophone, the trumpet, and the singer with the shaved head, his voice ringing out in the Munich night that was still new to me. I could pick out the sound of her oboe as tenderness in the midst of conflict, plaintiveness at the height of pleasure, music straight from the records that first helped me shed my shell and introduced me to my gift. I followed the sound without realizing it. Behind the instrument, she was all in black, which suited her fair skin and her hair, which was short like a little kid's. She moved like a feather, her thighs merely imaginary borders of an infinite entity. She was the only foreign musician in a Moroccan rai band, as far from the other musicians as possible, and she was nearly blind to us, the audience. She walked around the space only when necessary, exhaling into her magical instrument without any sense of the difference and avoiding eye contact, and if one of us happened to bump into her, she smiled politely, contentedly, which only made her seem more absent. I dared to chase her, following her from corner to corner. I can still hear her music, Mariam. It was as pure and clear as if she were a soloist, even though she wasn't. She might've been there with us, but she played from some faraway place. For two hours, she didn't even dip her toes into the sea of life.

I pushed through the crowd and walked up to the bar, feeling the need to pursue her till my last breath.

I couldn't get over the idea that she'd come from some higher plane than Egypt or Munich. Somewhere with people like us but more attractive. . . . I decided all at once that I would do whatever it took to get close to her that night. To talk to her and tell her what happened to me when I saw her. I watched the dancing but didn't dance. Men tried to draw me into conversation or onto the dance floor, and I scared them off with a look. The idea of killing everyone who stood in the way of my meeting her felt like the ultimate justice. I tried to record the scene in my mind, second by second. Looking around for a piece of paper to write on, or at least a pen, I cursed myself for suddenly deciding to write seventeen years after I'd learned to read. I was in the last place on earth where I'd find writing implements: a bar, surrounded by drunk people. Now do you understand why Sara wrote letters to Michel? I turned inward and begged: *Come on, don't fail me now. Forget the suffering, just remember the number of singers around her, the shape of the instruments* . . . I went to extremes, tracing with my thoughts the audience's clothing, how many people were there, their body language. *Remember this—record it—tuck it away for years of drought. . . .*

I moved with the agility of a criminal and the slyness of a fox. I was in no hurry for the concert to end. I could pick out the oboe from the million other sounds the way you might pick out a hair from dough. I isolated it and held it in my daydreams like there was no other sound on earth, and when the concert ended, my heart skipped a beat, and I was thrilled. She put away her oboe, the snake she'd used to charm me, and I followed her when she left the bar. She spread her umbrella like a roof over her head, and as she advanced into the street and walked off like everyone else, I asked myself how she could move so easily without recognizing me. She never made the mistake of looking back over her shoulder to acknowledge me. Then the long walk took over my thoughts. I was happy and wished it would go on forever and that my life would waste away. So what if it did? The moment she couldn't stand the cold anymore and flipped up her coat collar, I tapped her on the shoulder and handed her my scarf.

Noémie stood in the middle of the street, eyebrows raised, and the rain surrounded us like a scene from a movie. I found myself sheltering with her under the umbrella. It happened naturally, without my intending to crowd her, and proximity gave me the right to admire her. I tried not to blink as I imagined the years of agony to come as her appearance was redistributed among all the women I met: the green eyes, the slender nose nestled deep in her skull, adorable little pores gathered around it like children. Unfortunately, I didn't have a camera to take pictures of her any more than I'd had a pen and paper to draw her with. Courage was the only weapon I had, and I gave her my name with all the fear that gripped me every time I tried to speak German: "Ich heiße Arwa." She narrowed her eyes at me and smiled as I wrapped the scarf snugly around her neck, pointing to my chest, borrowing a tenth language that might connect us. "Arwa." I started annoyingly repeating it: "Arwa, Arwa, Arwa." After a few seconds, she returned the greeting with a composed nod. I think the warmth of the scarf made her lower her eyebrows. I was just a woman, after all, and I couldn't hurt her, so what about me was frightening? When I didn't move, she was forced to introduce herself, too: "Je m'appelle Noémie." She was French, and I was back to where I started. The seconds slipped past as she looked at me curiously, and because she worried about me in the cold rain—due to gratitude for the scarf and nothing more—she said that if I wanted, I could keep walking with her. We walked in silence, Mariam, and my mind was a total blank. I would smile at her if she looked at me from the corner of her eye, questioning and embarrassed by her question. I would smile with confidence that the answer was written all over me but that she wouldn't read it. We walked for an hour, and I ended up winning a major victory: she no longer perceived me as a threat, and after some cajoling, she let me carry the oboe. Then I went further and took her hand in mine.

The hotel she was staying in was nondescript. You had to climb four steps and wipe your feet on the red doormat at the threshold, like the sign asked. Of course—Noémie didn't have Salah El-Adl's money. That's why she hadn't reserved a room near me on the banks of the Isar. The important thing for now, though, was getting out of the rain. Honestly, Mariam, I was planning to deliver her to the door and make sure she had a safe place to sleep, then head out again. I mean, what was I hoping for? When she invited me upstairs with her, she followed up the request with my name, a casual "Chère Arwa," and offered me a drink to chase away the cold. I didn't say no, but she entreated me anyway, and her warmth was genuine as she looked at my wet clothes with a frown. I told her in Arabic, "I'm not cold, but I'll come up." I was convinced she'd understand me and didn't double check. She wasn't from Munich but was French, from a suburb of Paris, and when morning broke, she'd go back there on the express train. She invited me to stay with her till she left, and I stayed.

On the stairs, her hand slipped from mine. There was a red rose lying on the table in the entryway. I regretted losing her hand, Mariam. With Noémie, I was making my way toward a fragility that wove its threads around me gently and turned me upside down. She patted the soft fabric covering her temporary bed as a sign that I should sit, and I sat, remembering the rose in the entryway and considering the similarities between it and Noémie. She pulled a can of beer from the fridge and settled next to me, her thigh touching mine as she drank and relaxed. She began to talk to me in simple sentences, as though retelling the story of the world after cutting out the fluff, and I listened without responding. I was receiving the language from one side as she drank and smiled, looked at me with kindness from the corner of her eye, turned away and lay down on her side like the rose on the table.

I fell in love with Noémie, Mariam.

She said her parents had a flower shop in France and that she helped out there on holidays. She'd rebelled against playing the oboe because she didn't like dress clothes. She liked the people in Munich; they seemed kind. "Where exactly is it, your country, Egypt?" She had a fiancé preoccupied with the principles of gardening and with agricultural facts, who claimed that the world without art would become more humane, and "I think he might have a point, but I kind of want to destroy the world. How about you?"

I was watching myself from above like I had the starring role in a film, and she was my co-star. She pushed back a stray lock of hair as she spoke, and I contemplated her, not missing a second. I didn't answer her question. Instead, I pulled out the oboe and handed it to her, by which I mean that I begged her to play, and she complied immediately. She sat up straight on the bed, earnestly, and enclosed the oboe in her lips, playing simply, as though she were in a church setting the sun ablaze. What was the name of the piece? I lay at her feet, worshipping, consecrating her body as the oboe swung between me and the emptiness of the street outside, where the rain had fallen silent.

She was still playing as I rose toward her, my body gliding like a fish being returned to the river. She was absorbed and sad, a wellspring of sorrow, and I was screaming her name on the inside, trying to ward away evil. The fact of the matter was that I had no right, no right to fight the world for her. She had a fiancé and a family, and Arwa had no relation to her and, on top of that, was basically homeless. She looked at me dead-on as the music from the wind instrument fissured before me, sharp as knives with no specific aim. As I stood there looking at her, a luminous thought struck me: the oboe was the answer; the oboe had *been* the answer my whole life. It was the only thing that could give me balance. Perhaps the thought lit up my face, and she finally surrendered and took notice of me, like no one else had. With abundant generosity and without a moment's hesitation, she offered me her magic flute: "C'est pour toi, Arwa." And, of course, Arwa accepted the gift.

In the morning, I said goodbye to her on the platform of the station I'd so recently arrived at, and she squeezed my hand and smiled, hiding the expression in her eyes. I watched her walk away, dragging her bags behind her. She didn't look back. Later, when they told me Salah El-Adl was being eaten up by cancer and wanted to see me before his soul left his body, I asked them to tell him two things: Arwa was now an oboe player busking in the public squares, and she dated women.

Cheer Up, Mariam, Cheer Up, Arwa

Nothing from the past can die. Even people who die will soon come back to life. They'll rise and talk about what they did and what was done to them. The corpses in the street and the quiet bullet. Even the silent walls will eventually talk about what happened in the house. They'll tell stories the way we do. When I came back, Mariam, my last hope was not to cry. If possible, I wanted to laugh, surrounded by people. To play music the way I needed to play it. To rewind the film reel of my life and edit it like the great directors. But before we woke up, you and I, in the same bed . . . for the first time in the same bed . . . I was singing for you in my dreams, a song about how it's soft and pale and beautiful. It repeats, "It's soft and pale and beautiful." I was touching you, and you were smiling and shy. Just like now. The two of us, we're all we have. Imagine if my life had continued in the cold the way it was supposed to. If, for a moment, I'd been content to sit in safety and hadn't taken any risks. If I hadn't stayed in the metro that day. If the soldiers hadn't beaten me or dragged me by my clothes. If they'd treated me with respect. . . . Imagine if our country was just. If the tanks hadn't crushed the Coptic protesters that day in front of the Maspero building. If they hadn't killed Michel twice and tried to do it a third time. If Sara hadn't risen up and told me to come back, no matter what she'd said before. Imagine. I wouldn't have traveled and come back and met you. I would never have felt the burning I feel against your body. Because of this skin that shivers, bristles, and sleeps, I'm chock-full of a vitality I never knew existed. Because of the lightheadedness and your terror of ecstasy. Our fear of our complete annihilation. Cracks appeared in your skin, and I thought how I should peel it away and extract the bone, then grind that down and use it as a wind instrument to distill your voice, pure, like God first created it, before erosion left its mark. By the dim light of love. By the distant light of the decrepit lamp in the living room. I discovered the truths of the universe one at a time and told you in silence, and you listened to me as only a kid can. The sun, Mariam, used to rise every day but without ever rising, and the moon cycled through its phases. The truth surprised me in my dreams: we're complete now. And I would never dare be satisfied with being complete.

The revolution is raging just a few steps away from us. Tomorrow I'll take you down there, fanning its flames, and letting it fan our own. Your land will never be lost to you again. In every position I came up with in bed, in the frenzy of ancient rhythms, and after life as we knew it ended, we heard heavy feet trudging up and down the stairs. It seemed to us that the furniture was shaking, that the fourth floor would collapse onto the third. We were still in bed, welded together in the darkness. You said that life here on Champollion was eternal and protected, and I believed you and peered through the windows at the neighbors' screens and the radio in the nearby café, which was broadcasting military marches. We were in Egypt and in the farthest place from it, both at the same time. It's true, Mariam. I've never in my life loved someone the way I love you.

At daybreak, Umm Kalthoum was singing "Amal hayati."

I moved about fixing up the place that I was sure seemed strange and uninhabitable to you, though I was sure my presence was reassuring. There was something desert-like about the scene, like the dirt piled up after deep excavations. It didn't suit you, Mariam. I thought about rearranging the living room. My thoughts raced. I was anxious because I hadn't made any food for you, so I said I'd go down to the street and buy something we could eat that would revive us. You sat down on the red chair and said it looked like an old slide you'd forgotten to tell me about, from when you were a kid. I called your name and held you, and the flavor of the hug surprised me. I was standing, holding you, your head resting against my stomach like in the dream. You sighed. When you asked me how such a modern chair had ended up in this old apartment, and why it was the color of gazelle blood, I answered that I'd bought it from a junk vendor who'd passed under the window yelling "Bikya! Robabikya!" about an hour before you'd appeared at the door. I didn't know where he bought it, or if he stole it from a house the police had raided. It felt like part of the new home we were going to build in the apartment on Champollion. I left the front door gaping open as I ran down the stairs, shouting, "Hey, man! Robabikya man!" I paid the first price he asked for it, and he beamed and wished me well. It wasn't an option for you to arrive, after all these years, and find me living in a museum.

Then you started out of my arms, your eyes widening, and asked, "Arwa, where's my phone?"

I ignored your question, obviously, like you'd never asked, and returned to my fussing about the house. Fix the antiquated water heater. Replace the pipes. This girl's delicate skin couldn't handle cold, polluted water. I deserted you as you were getting down off your regal red slide, talking to yourself, and then I saw something click. Your footsteps headed toward the bedroom as you looked for your phone, and it infuriated me that you had the presence of mind to do that. I needed something to light the stove with. Matches or a lighter . . . two stray stones . . . one stone split in half. I'd just remembered that the rest of the cash in my wallet was in euros and I'd need to make some kind of deal with the grocer, when you appeared again, annoyed, and said, "My phone's broken, Arwa."

The apartment on Champollion hadn't been maintained for years. The paint on the bathroom ceiling was faded and flaking off in fragile blotches that now began to fall onto my head and yours. I counted the years in my mind and answered your question with a question: "What do you need your phone for, Mariam?"

"The phone had the message on it, Arwa."

"What message?"

I smiled guiltily, feeling my heart break a little because of what I'd done. *Okay, but the message and the person who sent it are here in your arms* . . . "You mean *you* broke it, Arwa?" I held you close, and your hand held the phone tightly like a barrier between us. At that exact moment, the broken water heater finally switched on, and we found ourselves standing in a rainstorm. Where could we possibly go from such a cinematic moment? We allowed ourselves to be soaked, unmoving, and then I asked you to follow me, and you did. I walked you to the kitchen. I could feel the fever rising to my brain and the effects of beer in my bloodstream, even though I hadn't drunk a drop. I tried to open the balcony door. I pulled you behind me and pressed your chest against my back, wrapping your arms around me. The flesh of our bare feet touched the balcony tiles. I could handle the cold, but you couldn't. I pried off the rotting garlic decorating the balcony with my fingertips and threw it down the air shaft between the buildings. "What now, Arwa?" A cat somewhere meowed, the sound dreadful, and I flinched. "Mariam, look at me. Did I already tell you that sometimes I can smell beer on you? Answer me—I want to hear your voice." "No, Arwa, you didn't." I cast my gaze like a rope to the ground at the bottom of the shaft, far from the cat's yowling. I told you, "Throw away the phone, Mariam. Now." And you obeyed.

For Arwa's sake, Mariam set aside her unease.

Last night, and the night before last. However many nights it's been, I've felt you every time like it was the first time. As we enjoyed ourselves, the hands of the clock raced. I sang you a song by Sayed Darwish that I was surprised to find I knew by heart, "Ana haweit wa entaheit." *I have loved and I'm done.* I promised I'd play it for you on the oboe. You have to learn to play, too. Tomorrow. We need to be on equal footing . . . You said you swore years ago that you would never so much as touch the instrument, and you wanted to make good on your oath. I was still feeling the effects of the beer. We cleaned the mirror over the sink, laughing and mocking it for insisting on showing us our faces, even after all these years. This mirror had witnessed horror upon horrors. Then came hunger.

I opened the door of the sad bedroom wardrobe, and it made a funny sound, but you didn't notice. I wished you'd noticed, Mariam. You were shivering from the cold, and I came close to wrap you in a green towel scented with jasmine. In the wardrobe, I also found some of Sara and Michel's underthings, and we sorted through them, feeling nostalgic. We need stuff for our home, Mariam. Food more than anything.

"But there's a revolution going on—who's going down there to look for food now?"

"Arwa will, Mariam. Who else? I'll go to the nearby shop and buy bread and cheese and tuna and water. I won't take long. I'll gather up everything I can find to eat, just grab it all and run. I won't pay, either, because that bill was paid ages ago. I'll remind the shopkeeper."

"You're going to leave me here alone, Arwa?"

"I'll leave you the oboe. Stand by the window. Keep fear behind you and the street in front of you, and wrap the little quilt around yourself to stay warm. Wait exactly two minutes, and then you'll see me again, over there, by the short row of tables at El Tak'eeba. I'll turn around and give you a wink. Be still, like the painting of the faithful Virgin. . . . And if I take too long, if it's too much, just pick up the oboe, hold it to your lips, and blow whatever tune comes to mind."

"I swore I wouldn't touch the oboe, Arwa, and it *will* be too much. I can't handle you being gone."

She covered herself in the quilt and pulled the throne over to the front door. She said she would press her ear to the door so as not to miss a single footstep while I was gone. All I had to do was hold it together and hum the tune that went, "If I'm content for him to go." Before I opened the door, we embraced, and Mariam cried into my chest. I was wearing the clothes I'd been wearing when I left Munich. It was very dark outside, and cold: I could tell from the pale faces of the people at the café. I made my way forward, resisting the drumming in my chest. History's a source of pain, Mariam. Pain is inherent to history. . . . I turned my back to Mariam in the lane before entering the shop. I had the euros in my pocket, as well as a few pounds. I felt the pangs in my heart worsen when I thought about what we would need to sustain a life together, and I calmed myself by looking back at her, yearning for me in the window. I could see her with her legs spread, calling me, and I was completely drunk on the image. I'll play it for you, Mariam, like I promised. *I have loved and I'm done.* And I'll teach you to play it. *But I promised myself I would treat the oboe as sacred.* Mariam, the oboe was how you summoned me. You asked God for me one Laylat Qadr. Remember?

When I entered the store, the young shopkeeper was smoking and watching the demonstrations on TV. The moment he saw me, he tossed his cigarette aside and came toward me as though to surrender himself. In a minute, I'll speak Arabic and disappoint him. How I love causing trouble, Mariam. I addressed you in my imagination, saying, *Look how generous the world is, habibti*—and then I heard it, the oboe playing in the window, and I was happy.

Those were ordinary days . . .

www.ingramcontent.com/pod-product-compliance
Lightning Source LLC
Jackson TN
JSHW020715090326
99038JS00001B/349
* 9 7 8 1 6 4 9 0 3 5 1 3 4 *